BY WITCH'S MARK

THE WITCHES OF PORTLAND, BOOK 9

T. THORN COYLE

Her bones vibrated inside of her. The pattern was set. Another pattern opposed it.

But was an arrogant man a match for a Goddess and a witch?

Witches and anarchists wove day into night, flow into chaos. Pattern met pattern. Life met death. Rising met falling. New met old.

The cunning, slender hounds were back, dark eyes rolling, mouths tinged with spit and red. She tasted him. His magic. His blood. He was wounded. Angry. She felt that in her breath and in her bones.

The virgin Goddess would take her due.

1

TEMPEST

Lower body swathed in a sheet and light blanket, Harry snored softly on the massage table as Tempest dug a sharp elbow into a particularly dense knot in his trapezius. He was always exhausted, and always way too tense. The perils of running a small non-profit, she supposed.

A random, chill lounge mix played softly from a speaker in the corner of dimly lit treatment room, competing with the soft tick of the radiant heater. It was damn cold outside —supposed to snow later in the week—but the room was warm. Couldn't have the clients getting cold. Tempest appreciated it, too. She was always freezing. Her long-sleeved black shirt was pushed up on her forearms, exposing the tattoos that swirled down her right arm. A hummingbird trailing a knot work ribbon from its beak. The bright disc of the sun. And around her pale, slender wrist, the hatch marks of the Irish alphabet, spelling out her name in ogham.

She'd been itching to get more ink and almost had enough saved up. Maybe she'd make an appointment soon. Give herself a Solstice gift. There was a spot above the ogham bracelet, on the soft skin above the tendons that fed into her fingers, calling out for something.

Maybe something to match the tiny pentagram inked inside her left wrist. Except for when she was working, it was usually hidden by a watch. Even though the small tattoo was protected on the inside of her arm, it still felt like a risk to tell random strangers that she was a witch.

Even though becoming a witch had given her purpose. Direction. A place to call home.

But that was private. Tempest didn't much like shouting anything about herself to the world.

She felt the knot give way. Harry's shoulder finally relaxed, descending from its spot beneath his ear.

Used to be, Tempest envied Harry's ability to sleep, but since she started taking CBD oil a month ago, her own sleep was getting a little better. Other things were shifting, too. As her constant exhaustion slowly decreased, she started to notice other, more subtle changes, as if her health itself might just be improving. It was too early to tell, but for the first time in ages, she dared to hope.

May Diana make it so, she thought. People were sometimes surprised that she was dedicated to Diana and not a more obvious healing deity. But Diana the Hunter was matron of Arrow and Crescent Coven, and that connection alone was good enough for Tempest.

Arrow and Crescent had saved her life. Well, Brenda had, really. Tempest had just left her last foster home—not a horrible place, just a place she needed to be free of for... reasons—and was looking for work and a place to crash. She'd stumbled into the Inner Eye.

Brenda had taken one look at Tempest, clucked, and within moments had a cup of tea in her hands and had tucked her into the little Tarot nook at the back of the store with the admonition to not move.

Tempest smiled and laid a gentle hand on Harry's shoulder. "Time to turn over."

He snorted with a start. "Uh. Yeah."

Besides, Diana was a healing Goddess, even if most people didn't realize it. She was often invoked to watch over a parent giving birth.

And she was the fierce protector of children. Tempest was down with that.

She lifted the sheet up by a foot or so while Harry muscled himself onto his side, flopped on his back, and scooched himself down on the sturdy table with a big sigh.

"Damn. I swear this is the only time I sleep."

"Then you must need a massage every day." Tempest pumped a shot of oil into her hands and slid her hands under his back to work that trapezius from a different angle.

Harry groaned. "If I could afford the time or money, believe me, I would."

Then his breathing slowed again as he drifted off.

Tempest deepened her own breathing to match the movements of her hands. She spread her bare toes on the carpet beneath the table and imagined her center of gravity sinking toward the earth. The energy work she'd learned from the coven coupled with her massage training were sometimes the only things that allowed her to function at all.

Her health had gotten really bad in the past year, and her coven mates had taken to shooting her worried looks. She was worried herself. There were days when she was barely functional. It felt as if she were half-drowning. Her brain didn't track and her body didn't want to move.

The worst part was, if Tempest couldn't get out of bed, she couldn't work. And that really wasn't good. She'd saved up two months of basic expenses—at her coven mate Alejandro's insistence and backed up by Brenda and Raquel, who wanted her to work on saving even more. But still, she was always aware of just how close she was to ending up on the streets.

She had been there before, too many times. Running from crappy foster parents after the first, decent family had moved out of state for work and decided not to adopt her and take her with them. She had really hoped for that.

Not getting it turned her further inward. Made her even less trusting than before.

For years, she imagined what it would be like if that family had made a different choice. If she'd gotten proof that someone valued her. Instead, it was just another loss. The sharp knife of grief, turning in her gut again.

She'd buried the anger and disappointment and kept going. Surviving.

Then she found Brenda, and by extension, the coven. So here she was, five years later, taking care of herself and surrounded by a small group that genuinely seemed to care.

She focused on sending healing energy as deeply into Harry's muscles as she could. That, and the scent of almond oil, helped soothe her worries.

But they didn't ever seem to go away.

RUBY

Ruby should be at home, packing stock and printing out price lists, but damn if she didn't need a break from worrying about her possibly-in-trouble business. Besides, punk shows didn't come along every night, especially not in December. The cider was crisp and the music—played at loud volume—shook her battered combat boots. She was starting to sweat in her waxed flak jacket and cranberry wool sweater. Almost time to shuck some layers.

She was in the cider-making area—the cidery—of the combination pub and distillery that was Cider Liberation. Two separate rooms, with a snug pub and games room up front, and a larger warehouse space attached. The cidery itself was filled with massive vats and barrels, all filled with cider at different levels of production. The operation took up half of a large, concrete floor, plus a mezzanine up top. The other half of the floor was left open for community meetings or concerts, like tonight.

The warehouse room of the cidery was packed with young adults like her, plus middle-aged punks and old trade unionists. Cider Liberation always attracted a mix of people from Portland's radical left. Anarchists and Marxists bought each other drinks and threw darts in the pub room, and slammed shoulders in the warehouse on punk nights or danced wild jigs when folk bands rolled through town.

Tonight, three middle-aged Black dudes shared the small cidery stage. Drums, bass, and lead guitar. They wore a strange but pretty badass combination of medieval armor and punk rock battle gear. Dreadlocks flying, their large, powerful bodies stomped out the rhythm, pounding the weathered boards with metal-capped boots. The lead guitarist grinned wildly and leaned into the mic, spitting rapid fire lyrics into the crowd. A cover of Renegades of Funk.

She stood a few bodies away from the mosh pit tonight, tucked up against the mezzanine stairs. The stairs were roped off, but the treads made a good place to stash a pint, plus it was nice to have something to lean against when you needed a break from the crush.

Ruby smiled. How could she not? Surrounded by comrades, listening to a dope combination of funk and punk, with a cider in hand.

And then she saw her. Bleached-out, white-blond hair. A tiny waif of a person with a backpack slung over her shoulders and a vintage leather jacket. A black- and yellow-striped scarf was wound a million times around her neck, all the way up to her chin, framing an elfin face. Must be a Hufflepuff. Or really into wasps. Her eyes were huge. Obsidian orbs in a sea of white skin.

There were dark shadows beneath those eyes, and Ruby couldn't help but wonder what had put them there.

She was Lawrence, a young dude with a flattop Mohawk, whom Ruby hadn't seen in an age. He was part of a small cadre of Black punk Portland skaters. He was also some sort of witch.

"Hey, Rubes!" Her head snapped toward the voice. It was her friend Daniel. "I'm surprised to see you out and about this time of year. I figured you'd be holed up in your toy shop with Santa."

He raised a pint glass filled with golden liquid. Someone bumped his shoulder, sending the cider cascading down the side of the glass.

"Sorry, man!" the person said.

"It's cool," Daniel replied.

They'd become friends a few years before. Despite the fact that their backgrounds couldn't be more different—she was working class Korean-American and his parents were Japanese and Jewish college professors—there just weren't that many Asian anarchists in the Portland punk scene. Everyone expected them to start dating but given that Ruby was only into girls and genderqueer folks and Daniel was strictly a cis het boy, Asian anarchists or not, that didn't quite pan out.

He was good people, though. Tonight, he wore his usual anarchist black. Battered coat, jeans, and regulation boots. It all matched his hair, which tonight stood up in short spikes all over his head. The only relief came from a ratty blue scarf Ruby knew was made by his younger sister when she first learned to knit. Underneath his militant demeanor, Daniel was a big softy.

He turned to her again. "So. Nice to see you. Finally!"

"I had to get out of the house," Ruby replied. "I've done nothing but work for two months, but have one more huge push this weekend, and needed a break."

"To taking breaks."

He tilted his pint glass toward hers. They clinked.

Daniel unzipped his coat and shoved the blue scarf into a capacious pocket, revealing an Iron Front T-shirt, the three classic red arrows that pointed down and to the left, beloved of anti-fascists. But in this case, the descending arrows formed a trident, or, more accurately, a pitchfork. The ring around the arrows read "Antifascist. Satanist. PDX."

Daniel was part of ASP, the local Satanist group who weren't the "we believe in Satan as an entity" types, but were more of the "we believe in separation of church and state, and in thinking for ourselves, and in human liberation, so we'll call ourselves Satanists to piss people off" variety.

Except Daniel *did* believe something and did some kind of magic. It didn't come up much, and Ruby wasn't really clear about it all.

She admired ASP's verve, and all of the community service they did, but felt like being a queer, Korean-American, punk artist was enough flying in the face of normalcy for one person. Her freak plate was full.

Ruby and Daniel leaned companionably against the stair railing, bobbing their heads to the music. When the song ended, Ruby set her pint glass down on the stairs and clapped as Daniel whistled loud enough to puncture her eardrums.

"Dang, dude. You have to whistle so loud next to my head?"

"Sorry." From the grin on his face, she could tell he didn't really mean it.

Ruby threw a light punch at his biceps.

"Asshole." She took another sip of crisp cider and caught another flash of that white-blond hair. "Hey, do you know that woman across the room?"

"Which one?"

"Near the door to the pub. Platinum blond. Small."

He scanned the room. "Oh! With Lawrence. You know him, right?"

Ruby nodded and waved her hand for him to continue.

He flashed that wicked grin again. "So impatient. Anyway, that's Tempest. She works part time at the Inner Eye. I go there sometimes to pick up supplies. She's cool. Kind of shy, though."

Tempest. Ruby filed the name away. "So, she's a witch or something?"

"Yeah. Part of a local coven. Arrow and Crescent. Bunch of activists. I'm surprised you haven't come across them before."

She'd heard of Arrow and Crescent Coven, and had seen some of them around, but while she'd show up at big actions with a few friends, she'd never been part of an organization or gone to any planning meetings. And in a crowd of a thousand people, with so much going on, it was easy to even miss your friends. But someone like Tempest? Ruby would remember if she'd ever seen her before.

"No. I know about the coven, but I'm surprised I've missed her out and about, if that's the crew she hangs with."

"Tempest doesn't make it out for many actions. Or anywhere else, really. Frankly, I'm surprised to see her here tonight. She works two jobs and the only place I ever see her is at the store."

That made sense, especially if she was shy. Ruby hadn't had a girlfriend in six months. Her last, Tara, was a receptionist with zero outside interests except sex, pizza, and clubbing. Not a bad combination, but once she started complaining that Ruby spent too much time on her business instead of on her, Ruby decided it wasn't worth it anymore. Any woman who didn't get her need to create and what it took to make a living at it wasn't worth her time. No matter how much she missed the sex.

Across the room, Tempest had ditched her backpack and was talking animatedly to Lawrence, small, pale hands making arcs in the air. Big eyes intense.

"So, she uses she/her pronouns?"

"Yeah. Cis woman. But I have no idea which way she swings. You'll need to ask." There was that grin. Wicked. She swatted his arm again, which sent another cascade of cider down the side of his pint glass. He shook it off his hand and grabbed a cocktail napkin.

"Hey!"

"Sorry." It was her turn for a fake apology. She did help clean up the mess, though.

Now she just needed to figure out her strategy. She couldn't just blunder up to a shy witch all full of brass and swagger.

Or could she?

Either way, she was going to drink more cider first.

3

TEMPEST

In the back of the big, noisy cidery warehouse, Tempest set her barely touched pint down on the small, sticky standing table she and Lawrence gathered around.

She wanted to stay. She'd thought listening to the band safely from the back of the room would work fine, but it turned out being in the back didn't help. It just meant she didn't have clear sight lines to the stage, and that boisterous bodies still danced too close for comfort. Tempest never thought of herself as claustrophobic until she couldn't see more than a foot or two in front of her face.

Mostly though? It was just too loud. Maybe she shouldn't have come out after all. Despite whatever boost the CBD oil was giving her lately, crowded, noisy places with no quiet corners to escape into still taxed her energy levels and made her introverted self crawl inside her skin. Not that she didn't enjoy the music. The three men on the small stage were really good. It was just all a bit too much.

Being in the overcrowded, noisy concert space was already taking a toll. A growing lethargy threatened to swamp her. Her body and emotions were beginning to retreat, heading toward shut down.

Damn. She really wanted to be able to get out and have fun, but she clearly needed to stick to smaller groups still. Being a shy introvert sucked sometimes. Add in chronic illness? She probably shouldn't be going out at all. But even *wanting* to go out was such a nice change, she'd jumped at Lawrence's invitation. It might have been a mistake, though.

The music was a rhythmic battering ram.

"You okay?" he shouted near her ear. He looked worried, with creased brows and a slight frown. "I thought this would do you some good. You spend so much time alone...but you're not looking so hot."

"It's just too loud," she got out. "Too much of everything, you know? I'm getting kind of tired."

"Psychic pressure?"

Yes. That was it.

It wasn't just the noise and the numbers of people—or her illness—it was that the people were all emoting, all at once. Thoughts and emotions flew through the air. All of it pressed on Tempest's sternum, making it hard for her to breathe. She hadn't been out in a crowd in so long, she'd forgotten to close down the edges of her aura against the onslaught.

Shy. An introvert. And an empath. Ugh. At least being an empath made her good at both of her jobs.

She and Lawrence leaned as close to each other as they could, so they didn't have to talk quite so loud.

"Can you help me? I need to shore up the edges of my aura, but..."

"But you're already too drained." He nodded. Since he started his private apprenticeship with Brenda, he'd learned a lot. Tempest was impressed. Maybe he'd join the coven someday. She hoped so. Lawrence was good people, and Arrow and Crescent could use another young person. At least, she thought so. It was nice to have someone near her own age to talk to about magic stuff. Someone who hadn't been studying it for eons.

"How about if I put up a temporary shield around you? Think you could re-center long enough to get your ætheric edges in order?"

"You can do that?" He must've learned even more than she'd thought.

He gave a half-hearted shrug and grimaced. "In theory. I've been practicing with Brenda, but you know, under quieter conditions."

Tempest laughed. "I know that feeling. May as well give it a go."

He set down his own pint glass, looked around, then nodded again.

"I know I should be able to do this stuff with my eyes open, but I'm not there yet. Try to find your center while I do this, okay?"

She swallowed and nodded. He closed his eyes.

Watching him sink into himself, seeing his chest slowly rise and fall, Tempest tried to slow her own breathing down. She tried to imagine energy flowing through the soles of her feet, connecting to the earth beneath the club, but she was having trouble sensing anything. She'd just have to pretend.

All magic starts in the imagination, Raquel had taught her during her apprenticeship with the coven. We imagine what we want first, then act.

And then she felt it. An almost audible snap around the outside edge of her aura. The music was still loud, but the push and clamor died away, as if lightly muffled in cotton wool. She relaxed with a sigh, and rolled her head on top of her neck, releasing muscles she hadn't even realized were that tense.

Eyes still closed, Lawrence gestured with his hands, as if to say, "Your move."

She leaned toward him again and said, "Okay. Your thing seems to be working. I'll give it a go."

Tempest reached for her own training, gathered her attention into the center of her head and, on a large exhalation, dropped it into her center. It popped right up again. Damn.

Again. She heard Brenda's voice inside her head. Tempest inhaled through her nose, imagining a still point in her belly. Then she imagined her consciousness as a ball in the center of her head, and, exhaling, imagined it dropping once again toward her core. This time, it worked. Her consciousness deepened. Broadened. Her breath flowed more easily. She breathed into her center, and she sent her exhalation out to the edges of her aura, to meet Lawrence's temporary shield.

She imagined her breath painting a shimmering layer along her outside edge, defining where her energy field reached out, marking a boundary anchored by the stillness in her center.

She gave it three long breaths, and felt her energy fields stabilize. She could do this. Every part of her remembered how. Opening her eyes, she touched Lawrence's hand. "I'm good."

He exhaled upward, sharply, then opened his eyes and smiled. She felt his energy receding from around her. Felt him gathering it back toward himself. Felt her own edges waver for a moment, then catch and hold steady once again. She smiled back.

"Better?"

"So much better. Thank you."

"Thank Brenda. Without her training, I wouldn't have been able to help you."

"Without her training and your practice," she pointed out. "You don't get that good that fast without putting in some serious time."

He tilted his head in acknowledgement, then picked up his pint glass and tapped it against hers.

"To practice," he said.

"To practice."

The place was still too loud and boisterous, but she couldn't feel every damn emotion flying through the room now. Huh. Maybe she wouldn't have to be such a recluse all the time. She could be, like, a normal early-twenty-something, at least, as much as a chronically ill witch could be called "normal."

Lawrence grinned at something over her shoulder.

"What?" she said.

"Don't look now, but I think someone's coming over to talk to you."

"What?" Tempest started to swivel around. Lawrence grabbed her wrist.

"Don't look! Wow. You really have no cool, do you?"

Tempest flushed. "No. I don't. Who is it?"

"Ruby. She's pretty great, actually. Kind of your polar opposite, but I think you might hit it off."

Ruby. She. A girl. Tempest groaned and looked up to see a gorgeous, broad-hipped, Asian woman navigating around the edges of the crowd. Beautiful dark eyes in a rounded, smooth-skinned face. Lips painted a luscious shade of red that brought heat to Tempest's cheeks. Really, really tight black jeans cuffed just above the tops of her battered combat boots.

Oh, boy.

Maybe the sticky floor would open up and swallow Tempest before this Ruby person got to their table.

"I still can't handle the noise in here," she said. "Can we head back into the pub?"

Lawrence smirked at her.

"Right. Too noisy." His voice was skeptical but teasing.

She knew she'd be in for an earful once they'd cleared the cidery door, but for now, it was enough that he picked up his pint glass and forged a path through the crush.

Maybe someday, with enough practice, Tempest would feel comfortable enough to talk to some random girl heading her way at a concert, but not tonight.

Tonight, just being here was enough.

4

RUBY

She was well fortified with cider and the band was still spitting bars from the stage. With a roll of her ample hips, Ruby felt her swagger kick in as she carved a pathway through the crowd, heading toward the doors leading to the pub, where Lawrence and the small, platinum blond—Tempest—had just walked through.

As soon as she got near the door connecting the two spaces, she heard a commotion from the other side.

"Nazis out! Nazis out!"

"Shit," she said, barreling through the doors. In the games space just off the pub, she half crouched behind a pinball machine.

The Patriots had arrived to fuck shit up, the way they did. Those assholes couldn't abide anarchists, communists, or queers having a good time. She really shouldn't be here, should turn around, get the plug pulled on the band, and get everyone out the back door. But she wanted to make sure Lawrence and Tempest were safe, first. The pub had already turned into a melee. Bodies scrabbled in a football scrum. One of the high-top pub tables was overturned. She saw a fist fly toward a face, which snapped backward. Hoarse voices shouted.

Shifting position to try to get a clear view, she stepped on something. Her foot rolled over her ankle, but she caught herself on the ball of her foot and moved her boot again. "What the—?"

It was a dropped dart. She pocketed it, really hoping she wouldn't need to use it, and hoping no one else thought to use the weighted darts as weapons.

The shouting and the music clashed around her. She really could not get into a brawl tonight. Not with tomorrow being such a big money day. Plus, she hadn't been to the boxing gym in months.

"Damn it!" She got as close to the scrum as she could without landing directly in the middle of it, using the low knee wall that separated the darts and pinball space from the rest of the pub as cover.

Then she saw a flash of white-blond hair in front of that flattop Mohawk hairdo. Lawrence. He was ferrying her out the door. Good. That meant Ruby didn't have to stay.

A foot shot out of nowhere, tripping Ruby to the ground. She slammed onto her forearms and knees, then rolled and turned. A tall man with wheat-blond hair with shaved sides was turning away.

Cursing her sore knees, she scrambled up and ran back into the cidery, pushed herself through to the woman running the sound deck and shouted in her ear.

"Patriots in the house!"

The woman grimaced, nodded, and cut the sound. The lead singer staggered to a halt and the crowd yelled out its disappointment. Ruby filled her lungs, reached up to her full height, and yelled.

"Patriots are in the house! Anyone who needs to get to

safety, head out the back door! Do *not* walk off alone!"

The crowd mobilized immediately, unfortunately used to the drill. Far too often over the past three years, the Patriots had initiated violence against the anti-fascists of Portland. In the last year, though—even as their numbers shrank almost to non-existence from community pushback and their own infighting—they'd grown even bolder, bringing the fight to home turf, as it were. Which sucked. Cider Liberation had been a safe space for them all. But lately? It felt as if there were fewer and fewer places left in Portland where folks on the edges could go.

She let a crew of folks pulling bandanas over their lower faces by. Let them join the fight to protect what should have been a safe space. Ruby couldn't risk it. She joined the people heading for the back door, making space for two red-shirted socialists in wheelchairs.

She just hoped the outdoor courtyard wasn't full of fascists.

It took all of her patience to remain a good comrade and not shove her way through to the door. Despite a bunch of training in street tactics, the animal part of her just wanted to get free. And she was still worried about the blond witch. Nothing to do about it, though, so might as well get herself to safety. The band was packing up and a chain of folks passed equipment toward the door. Good. That must mean the courtyard was safe for now, or they wouldn't risk it.

She followed the small, roiling crowd toward the back of the cidery, wishing that her fun night out had ended with her meeting a cute new girl, instead of in the middle of another fucking mess.

Yeah, and liberty and justice for all.

Ruby grabbed a snare drum from the stage and headed toward the door.

5

———

TEMPEST

The Inner Eye was still a refuge to Tempest. Her home away from home. While her tiny apartment above Joshua's garage was her own private nest, Brenda's shop was the first place she felt safe in her late teenage years. It was still the place she wanted to be when upset, and last night had upset her. The angry crowd brought back all of her old fears. The violence that split the air when the so-called Patriots arrived at the pub still crackled at the edges of her aura. It took all of her attention to keep herself together.

Luckily, today was a workday at the shop anyway. If it hadn't been, Tempest would have likely found some excuse to make her way here. She was supposed to go with Lawrence to a craft fair when she got off work, but she just wasn't sure she felt up to it.

Maybe the lift she'd gotten from the CBD wasn't real. After last night, she felt almost knocked back to the way she was a few months before. Oh, still more functional, but dang, she was tired.

Trying to calm her soul, Tempest hummed along to Wendy Rule's *Persephone* album as she dusted the shelves.

She'd barely squeaked through her morning meditation and stretches, before choking down some oatmeal and heading in to work. As soon as she'd arrived and told Brenda what had happened at the pub, Brenda had smudged her aura with a bundle of lavender, chamomile, and rosemary. That had helped, but Tempest felt as if she needed a second round.

Nothing bad had happened to her because Lawrence had gotten her away in time, but the whole situation still unsettled her.

"You doing better?" Brenda came up next to her, arms filled with books needing shelving. The older woman set the stack down on one of the small tables nestled between comfy reading chairs in the book section of the store. It was one of Tempest's favorite jobs, shelving books filled with information her teenaged self only dreamed of having access to.

She shrugged in response, cheating a glance up at her mentor before lowering her eyes back to her dusting. She could feel Brenda's gaze, and knew her boss's blue eyes were trained on the top of her head.

Tempest sighed, set down the duster, and met Brenda's gaze. Her eyes didn't look worried, which was good, and her presence calmed down Tempest's animal soul. The thing that coiled inside of her, tense and ready to spring, relaxed its vigilance a little. Brenda's brown hair was up today, in a messy bun that spiraled loose curls around her face. She wore a turquoise sweater tunic over black leggings and black knee-high boots. A large moonstone caught the light at her breastbone, and her wrists were covered in silver bangles.

Brenda not only looked like a witch, or spiritual teacher, she was also one of the wisest people Tempest knew.

Tempest trusted her more than she trusted anyone, but that didn't mean the distrustful parts of her went away. Especially not after last night's scare.

"Do you need a break? Or some more tea?"

Tempest looked around the shop. A few people browsed near the front shelves, looking at Tarot cards and stones. Saturday customers always came in waves, and the shop was in a lull for the moment.

"I honestly don't know what I need," she finally replied. "Do you?"

Brenda gestured at the two stuffed reading chairs. "Let's sit down for a bit. I'll keep an eye on the customers while you talk."

Tempest sank into one of the chairs and crossed her left ankle over her right knee, forming the glyph of Saturn. She was just learning astrology and figured invoking the planet of stability wasn't a bad idea right about now.

"That's right," Brenda said. "Stability. Earth. Form. Breathe into your center."

Tempest followed her high priestess's instructions. Oh, Arrow and Crescent didn't go in for titles, but for her, Brenda and Raquel both would always hold that title, at least in Tempest's heart and mind.

The breathing helped. Just sitting near Brenda helped. But the uneasiness Tempest had felt while working with her massage client hadn't fully left. The events at Cider Liberation, while they didn't feel exactly connected, sure hadn't helped. And now that she thought about it, the uneasiness had started at least a few weeks ago. Just after the last full moon.

"It's just so hard to not run and hide," she finally said. "To disappear. I mean, I don't want to, but at the same time, I do. Does that make sense?"

Brenda nodded. She sat comfortably, yet looked regal, like some sort of New Age queen.

"It does. You've lived through trauma, Tempest, and your animal soul is fighting with your rational consciousness. Your mind knows you're safe now, but the more childlike, instinctive parts of you don't believe it." She tapped one beringed finger to her lips. Thinking. "But while I think that's a large part of it, I also don't think that's all. I know you don't believe it yet, but you've come leaps and bounds in your psychic training. Looking at your aura, it seems to me that you may actually be picking up on something."

Tempest sagged back in her chair, relief at hearing Brenda say those words out loud easing some of the tension vibrating through her body. "Really? It's not just me, being weird?"

Brenda threw her a look at that but didn't school her for talking down about herself like she usually would. She shook her head, long earrings swinging beneath errant coils of hair. More moonstones dangled at the ends. Tempest thought Brenda's partner, Caroline, was a lucky woman to be with such a powerful, gorgeous witch. Tempest herself was never sure if she had a crush on Brenda or wanted to grow up to be like her someday.

You need to grow into yourself, Brenda would say. And yeah, that was fine for someone who had her life together. But at twenty-three years old with one foot off the streets? Tempest still felt like a wreck.

"What does it feel like, inside you?" Brenda asked.

Tempest took another deep breath and dropped into her center, just like she'd been trained to do. From there, she cast her attention through the rest of herself, and the space around her, seeking information, trying to sense the answer to what Brenda was asking.

"It feels as if there's something bad out there, waiting, biding its time."

"Biding its time for what?" Brenda frowned.

Tempest breathed into the sensation. Letting her awareness sink even deeper inside herself, she followed the information her whole being sought out. Tempest was what was called "clairsentient." Her main psychic conduit came through her body. Her coven mate Tobias said that was probably why she took to massage so easily. She was naturally good at finding pain in people's bodies and could intuit how to release that pain. And he was right. Massage school had been one of the first things in her life that Tempest had found easy, and the longer she was in practice, the more certain she became of herself.

Even battling her chronic illness, she did pretty well with massage, and with her part time job here at the Inner Eye, taking care of all the physical stock. She wasn't always so good at reading the customers from a distance, the way Brenda could, but she was getting better at that, too. At least she thought she was.

Until the uneasiness crept in. And doubt followed the uneasiness, along with the voices that told her she'd never amount to much, and that people only tolerated her, not loved her. And that if they *did* love her? Well, that just meant sooner or later they'd leave her.

Stop it, she told herself. *Follow the energy, the way Raquel and Brenda taught you.*

She closed her eyes, gathered her scattered attention, and dropped back into sensing.

Where was it? What was it? The sick tension seemed to have a single locus. It was pointed. Focused. But where was it coming from?

"Are the customers okay?" she said out loud. "Is it okay if I go deeper?"

She heard Brenda's bracelets jingle as she shifted. "They're fine. Only one person in the shop right now, and I put up a *come back in ten minutes* shield over the door."

"You can do that?" The words burst out of Tempest's mouth before she realized how ridiculous they were. Of course, Brenda could do that. Tempest waved a hand as if to flap the words away. Brenda gave a soft laugh.

"Do what you need to," she said.

Tempest nodded and dropped into her subconscious like a stone falling into a dark well.

6

———

RUBY

Ruby had helped the band load out and gotten a few other people safely to their cars before getting a two-person escort to her car sometime around eleven. She'd collapsed onto the sofa and had a whiskey with her house-mates before calling it a night.

And now? She was in a huge hotel ballroom near the Portland Conference Center in the midst of an interlocking Venn diagram of hundreds of geeks and craftspeople.

Geeks and Bells was her favorite event of the year. Not only was it fun and festive, with some really unusual crafts, she also made enough money to pay her rent for several months and restock her craft supplies. After the year she'd had, she hoped that was true this time. If it wasn't? Woven Magic was in serious trouble. Business had been in a serious slump all year.

Her booth looked good. It was filled with bright colors. Hand woven shawls, scarves, and small wall tapestries hanging from the booth walls and wooden dowel rack displays on top of her two tables. Along with the regular stuff she sold at every craft fair she attended, for this event, Ruby busted out all of her geek specific weaving.

She had red and gold scarves with lightning bolts woven in. Green with a lantern shape. Long, black-and-white neck scarves with stormtrooper heads woven into each end. Flip the scarf, and it was a black Darth Vader helmet. She also featured the simple Zelda Hyrule crest, My Little Pony candy-colored scarves with a curl of mane woven over black eyelashes, Fortnite grenades...on and on. If it was geeky and she could weave it, Ruby did her best.

Mass produced geek scarves or wall tapestries had pictures printed shoddily on top of the weave. Hers were the only ones with symbols actually woven in.

So far, the weekend's sales were doing a lot to make her feel better about the night before, especially since she had lost track of that adorable witch. She'd never even gotten to meet her.

"Damn fascists," she muttered. "Blocking my game."

"What's that?" A tween in coveralls, Afro, and a pink hoodie looked up from the woven bracelets they were fingering with longing and looked at Ruby. The least expensive thing Ruby carried, she tried to make the bracelets in as many different geeky color combos as possible.

"Nothing!" Ruby said brightly. "Just muttering to myself. You into Sailor Moon?"

The tween kept coming back to a pale-blue-and-white bracelet with thin lines of red and yellow woven through.

The tween nodded.

"Tell you what, you can have that one, if you tell your friends where you got it."

"Really?" The kid's brown eyes grew huge. "You'd do that?"

"I would. Here"—she picked up the slender weaving—"hold out your wrist."

The tween held out their left wrist, shoving the hoodie sleeve up on a thin brown arm.

Ruby wrapped the bracelet twice around before tying it securely.

"Remember, I'm Woven Magic. Okay?"

"Thanks, lady!" The tween raced off, tugging on the sleeve of an adult who looked completely frazzled since they seemed to be in charge of a motley crew of at least five other twelve-year-olds, some wearing Fortnite T-shirts, Pokémon gear, or D&D backpacks. Ruby was glad that D&D was still around. She'd spent most of her middle school years deeply embedded in one campaign or another, and still played every other month or so.

She went back to straightening stock and wondered if she should text Lawrence and ask him about Tempest. Ruby sighed. She hadn't seen Lawrence in a while. For all she knew, he'd broken up with his former girlfriend, though that would've been really dumb, and taken up with the adorable witch. Or more likely, Ruby's gaydar was on the fritz and the girl was straight as an arrow.

Maybe she'd just leave it up to fate or whatever force governed geeky queer girls' lives. All she knew was, she hadn't had sex in almost six months, and that shit was getting old.

A tall, skinny white dude, hair shorn high and tight except for a long, wheat-blond sweep that dangled over his angular face, dressed in the obligatory black T-shirt, black jeans, with a black winter coat slung over one arm, approached the booth. Something about the way he carried himself was familiar, and set Ruby's teeth on edge, but if she refused to sell to every geek who squicked her, she'd be out of business.

Oh. Great. A heavy silver upside-down pentagram dangled from an equally heavy silver chain around his neck. She doubted very much that he was part of Daniel's ASP group of anti-fascist, mostly-non-theistic Satanists. But maybe she should give him the benefit of the doubt.

"You part of ASP?"

His lip actually curled. Dang. "No. I prefer a more traditional path."

"Cool," she replied. Not cool, though. Her spidey senses were really tingling and she just wished he'd go away. But until he did something rude, he could browse. But she still hated that he pawed at the merchandise.

People pawing the merchandise was part of how she sold things. The colors and patterns drew them in, but it was the weight and texture that secured the sale. Ruby's work was quality, and touching it was all the proof a person usually needed.

"Got any *True Blood* merch?" he asked.

"Like, vampire stuff? I've got this gorgeous red-and-black shawl patterned with roses and thorns."

She slid her hands beneath the shawl. She wasn't lying. The thing was actually gorgeous, and any Goth or would-be vampire worth their salt circle would love it. She held it up so he could see, but he was already shaking his head.

"No. I meant more of werewolf stuff. You know, like the wulfsangel."

Anger flashed through her body. *Damn it. I have to trust my fucking intuition.*

"Get out," she said softly.

He held up his hands, smirk on his face.

"What? What's wrong with the wulfsangel?"

The wulfsangel had a long history. It started as a physical wolf trap, morphed into a symbol of peasant revolt, and was then adopted by the Nazi party before becoming an ill-considered emblem of a werewolf cadre on the popular TV show.

But yeah. It was mostly used by Nazi assholes.

"I don't sell to fascists," she replied, carefully setting the shawl back on the table. "Get out."

"You have no right!"

"I do," she replied. Scanning the aisle, she caught the eye of her friend Sean, a huge blond bear of a man who sold carved wooden toys. He nodded, bent to say something to his partner, Carla, a woman with frizzy brown and silver hair. She glanced up from the display of carved spinning tops, worried dark eyes darting between Ruby and the skinny dude. Sean flexed his fingers, rolled his shoulders, and started over.

Skinny white dude followed her sight line, put down the Slytherin scarf he'd been handling, and stepped away from the booth.

"Fuck you," he said, then turned and walked away.

Sean followed him five steps, until the guy turned at the corner booth two spaces down.

"You okay?" Sean asked, walking back to her table.

"I'm fine. Thanks for coming over. Just an asshole wanting Nazi symbols, acting like a *True Blood* fan. He seemed like he was going to make trouble."

"Ugh. I thought we'd run those dudes out of town. Bad pennies, every last one of them. I'll call security, tell them to be on the lookout."

"Thanks, Sean. I owe you a beer."

He grinned. "You don't, but I'll take you up on it, anyway. After we close tomorrow?"

"You're on. Carla, too."

"If he comes back, you have my number."

He ambled off, phone held to his ear.

She looked down the aisle, unable not to look at where the skinny fascist had been.

The only thing she saw was a crowd, ebbing and flowing, stopping at booths, laughing, holding out credit cards.

And then, a horde of tweens descended on her booth.

"Hey, lady! We walked around some, but I brought them back! See!"

"I do see! Thank you!" She gave the kids a huge smile, allowing their enthusiasm to drain away some of her stress and anger. "What can I show you guys?"

Part of her attended to her new customers, helping them pick out just the right colors for their bracelets. She really loved nothing more than helping geeky kids.

But in the back of her mind, she couldn't help but hope the tall, skinny man was long gone.

7

———

TEMPEST

Only half aware that her body was still in a comfortable chair in the bookstore area of the Inner Eye, Tempest traveled.

The darkness her spirit moved through felt familiar. Safe. Tempest felt the pentagram tattoo inked on the soft skin beneath her left wrist begin to tingle.

The first tattoo she'd gotten after joining Arrow and Crescent, Selene had teased Tempest about her "witch's mark" and then had to explain what a witch's mark was. A mole or wart or other mark on the skin, witch's marks were used as "proof" that a person was consorting with demonic forces. They often sent people—mostly women and gay men—to their deaths.

Some contemporary witches, Selene explained, reclaimed the concept of being marked as a way to say "piss off" to a culture that wanted them to behave or live a certain way.

Tempest just liked tattoos and could only afford the smallest ones possible. She'd also wanted to mark her new journey.

Over time, as Tempest's powers grew, she found that the pentagram tattoo in particular *was* magical. While the ogham bracelet connected her to herself, the pentagram connected her to her witchy nature because that's what it meant to her. At least that's what Brenda said. So, she supposed she had a witch's mark after all.

Tempest believed in the connection to witchcraft the tattooed symbol of the pentagram gave her, so she trained herself to respond to the tattoos and vice versa. Her rational mind couldn't explain it, but over time, she'd just learned to trust.

And she trusted it now.

"What's happening?" Brenda's voice was soft.

Tempest swallowed, tongue thick with the deep relaxation that came with this sort of psychic work.

"Pentagram tattoo. Tingling. Something's up. Gonna follow it."

"Stay with it," Brenda said. "I'll be right back."

Tempest was aware of Brenda moving past her. A thought darted through her mind—*Must be taking care of that customer*—but was just as quickly gone. Her tattoo seemed to be pointing toward the west, so wandering through the darkness, she headed that direction.

She trusted that if anything really bad happened, Brenda would bring her back. *If she finishes ringing up that customer in time.*

Oh, hush, she told her scaredy-cat voice. She imagined a pale beam of moonlight shining in her heart. The light of the crescent moon. The light of Goddess Diana. It would guide her on her way.

Tempest was further away from her center than she'd been since she started studying witchcraft. She'd grown used to sticking close to home, so to speak. Mostly because that's what the coven suggested for all dedicants, or people newly dedicated to the coven, but not full initiates yet. But she also stuck close to home because of the sense of safety it offered her. As a foster kid, finding home was a precious thing.

But the tattoo insisted, and so did her intuition.

She journeyed on, following the slender moonbeam. Scenes flashed before her as she moved, shifting and changing as quickly as the mists that rose off the Willamette.

Scenes from the night before, when those angry people stormed the pub. There were symbols around them. Letters. Runes. Crooked-armed solar crosses.

Her heart pounded in fear.

Just as quickly as they arose, they were swept away again.

There was an image of the coven, doing magic in Raquel's attic. Was it the upcoming Solstice? It had the feeling of future, not past, though she could not explain why. Selene's moon-pale face looked up, startled, as if she saw Tempest somehow.

That scene faded, too.

And then, there was the image of a tall, skinny man with white skin and blond hair. Not platinum like hers, a true golden blond. He should have been beautiful but wasn't. His face was twisted with arrogance. Behind him, emblazoned on a black wall, was a massive, upside-down pentagram, glowing red. The faint outline of the downtown city skyline was embossed behind the pentagram, on the black wall.

He turned and stared, with knowing eyes. Her breath caught in her throat.

And then Tempest was falling, falling, falling. Her limbs

flailed, trying to slow her trajectory, desperately attempting to correct her course.

She thought of the shop. The bookcases. Brenda. The smells of incense and rose water. The comfortable chair.

That was enough. She felt the tug of body to spirit and floated gently down. She imagined stepping back into her body, and, on a huge, shuddering breath, settled all the way back in.

The scent of lemongrass made her nose wrinkle.

"Tempest." Brenda's voice. "Here. When you're ready, open your eyes and drink this."

Her eyes fluttered, blinking in the light. She heard cars on the street outside. People talking. The small fountain that burbled next to the cash register. Stretching her arms over her head, she arched her back until it popped, then lowered her arms on a whoosh of breath.

Finally, she looked at her mentor, who beamed at her as if Tempest was a very clever child.

"That looked like quite a journey," Brenda said, handing her a pale green ceramic mug filled with the pale gold tisane. "There's honey in there to help bring you all the way back."

Sugar in something warm was good for all kinds of shock, including the shock of allowing your consciousness to traverse strange places, far from your physical form.

Tempest sipped the brew, and *mmmed* in appreciation.

"Tobias gather these?" she asked. He was the other healer in the coven.

"Actually, I did," Brenda replied. "Good?"

"Good."

Brenda let her drink in silence for a moment or two. "So, what happened?"

"Well, first I saw the people from last night. They were

so angry. And there were symbols...like the kind those assholes who attacked Raquel and Zion used."

Brenda's lips pressed together in a thin line. "Well, we knew we weakened them badly, but figured a few of them had just crawled under a rock for the time being. I'm sorry to hear that they're back."

"Yeah. But that's not the part of the vision I'm worried about."

"What else did you see?"

Tempest looked across the store, eyes roaming past statuary, woven hangings, tumbled stones and herbs, not seeing any of it.

"There was the coven. And this is the weird thing...it seemed like we hadn't had that meeting yet."

"Like it was in the future?"

"Yeah. This coming Solstice, it felt like. Selene saw me, I think. It was weird." Tempest hunched her shoulders up and gave a little shake before dropping them again. She drank more herbal tea. "Do you think my psychic power is changing?"

"It seems likely. You've tended to be clairsentient, like most healers, but that doesn't mean you don't have clairvoyance and a little precog thrown into the mix. Most of us aren't any one thing. We're just stronger in one form than another."

Tempest nodded. She knew that, at least intellectually, but...

"And then there was the thing I really think I was meant to see." *The thing I don't want to tell you.*

"I heard that." Brenda's smile was rueful. "So just tell me anyway. Rip the bandage off. It's better that way."

"I saw a man. Tall. Skinny. A white man. And he was in front of a huge red upside-down pentagram."

"Like the Horned God pentagram? Or spirit descending into matter?"

Tempest waved a hand. "No. None of the things we work with. Satanic. And not in the good way, you know? Not the 'friendly neighborhood Satanists just trying to shake up the status quo.' Like, he seemed really, really bad."

"And?"

"And the pentagram was inscribed on top of the city skyline, which was bad enough, but…"

She looked at Brenda, whose blue eyes met her own. The moonstone at her breast winked in the shop lights.

"I think he's gunning for the coven. I can't explain why I feel that, but right before I left to come back, it seemed like he saw me, too. And he recognized me."

8

RUBY

Her enjoyment of the day diminished, Ruby put a smile on her face and pretended to get back into the spirit of things. Damn it.

Don't let the haters bring you down, she thought. But it was hard not to. Not knowing there were people like that guy everywhere, hard as the community fought against them, and despite recent victories that had kicked the fascists in the teeth.

She swore, they were like roaches.

A gaggle of Star Trek geeks walked by, shooting each other with tiny keychain lasers. While that coaxed a small smile from Ruby, it didn't interrupt her tumbling thoughts.

That's just it, though. She straightened her stock and replenished the woven bracelets that the tween crew had picked through. We have these small victories, but these days? They just don't seem to last. It's still one damn thing after another.

The smell of pepperoni pizza broke through her reverie, and her stomach reminded her she never took a lunch break.

"You okay, Rubes? Looks like you're about to glare a hole through that shawl there."

"Daniel! You didn't tell me you were coming!"

She turned to offer him a hug and stopped. Standing next to him was Lawrence with his distinctive flat-top Mohawk. And the adorable blond witch, dark eyes flicking up, and then down again, looking as if she wanted to sink into the hideous hotel carpeting. A blush stained her milk-pale cheeks with rose. That just made Ruby want to kiss her.

"Well, we didn't really get much chance to go over plans once all hell broke loose last night."

Ruby's brow creased. "Did you all get home safe?"

Adorable Witch nodded. Lawrence looked from her to Ruby, then spoke.

"I got Tempest out before things got too bad, and we walked to the bus with a few other folks. Got home fine. You?"

"Oh, yeah. I helped the band out, escorted some folks to their cars, and got an escort myself. How about you, Daniel? Looks like you got cut?"

A tiny red bandage graced his right temple. Glancing down, Ruby saw that the knuckles on his right hand were red and abraded. No broken skin there, at least.

"Yeah, I got caught in the melee after you ducked back in to help the band."

"Meaning, you went into the pub," Ruby answered, voice dry.

"I couldn't let Sam and his staff deal with those assholes alone. Besides, there were more of us than there were of them."

"Thank the Gods," Lawrence chimed in. "That's a welcome change, at least."

Ruby had to agree. The witch was inching her way

behind Lawrence, hands gripping her backpack straps, looking as if she wanted to disappear. Ruby stepped around Lawrence and held out her hand.

"We never got to meet last night. I'm Ruby."

Impossibly big eyes looked up from beneath the platinum-blond shock of hair. A quick swipe of a tongue over pale rose lips, and half a nod, as if the woman had come to an internal decision of some sort.

Then, a small pale hand reached for Ruby's larger, slightly darker one. Her skin was smooth and warm.

"Tempest," she said.

"Pleased to meet you, Tempest." Ruby held her gaze for just a moment, before turning to Lawrence. "And we've met before, but it's been a while. Lawrence, right?"

"Yeah." He shook her hand. No hesitation there.

"We were about to grab some food. Can we bring you something?" Daniel asked.

"I'd murder a slice of vegan pizza." Ruby loved meat, but dairy was a big no-no. "Or if you can wait, the floor closes in twenty and I can join you off site."

Daniel turned to Lawrence and Tempest. "What do you think? Seems like if the floor is closing that quick, we should get our shopping done anyway."

"Sounds good to me," Lawrence replied.

Tempest nodded. "Fine."

"Great. I could use a drink, anyway," Ruby said. "A fascist stopped by right before you all arrived. I need to wash the taste of that out of my mouth. Meet you outside the hotel in thirty."

Daniel's head snapped toward her, eyes sharp with concern. "Are you okay?"

"Yeah. I got backup, and sicced security on them. I just

hate that they were here, pawing at my stuff. A crappy Satanist wannabe, too."

9

TEMPEST

They were crammed into a booth at a phô place near the hotel. Tempest knew that most people wouldn't think that four to a booth was crammed, but when one of them was the hottest person Tempest had seen in a year, and Tempest wanted to crawl under the table, it sure felt crowded.

Why in Diana's name had she let Lawrence convince her to come to the craft fair at all? And then out to dinner? Augh.

Ruby was one of those people who were lit up inside. Animated. Glowing with some inner fire that Tempest never dared to have. She felt a flash of envy at Ruby's ease with people. At her high visibility. Her red sweater, punk boots, big jewelry, and easy smile.

And the way a hint of sex boiled underneath. Tempest bet even people who would swear Ruby wasn't their type had second thoughts when they met her.

Tempest never felt safe enough to be that visible. What must it be like?

And what would it be like to have someone like that as a

girlfriend? For that matter, what would it be like to have anyone as a girlfriend? Tempest had barely even kissed anyone, let alone anything else.

"So yeah, Daniel, I figured you should know there is someone out there at least pretending to be a Satanist who's up to no good."

"What did he look like?"

Ruby described a tall, skinny white man dressed in black. "He had one of those classic fascist haircuts. The military high and tight, but long on top. Wore an upside-down pentagram."

Tempest's ears perked up. That description. It couldn't be... Her clairvoyant skills weren't *that* good yet, though she'd been working on them. Being a clairsentient empath came naturally, with all the advantages and disadvantages. And before her training? The disadvantages outweighed everything. The rest of the psychic skill set, though? Not so much. She'd been working on them tooth and nail, determined to get better. It didn't matter how much her coven mates told her that everyone's skills were different, and that hers were just fine—Tempest couldn't help but think that being a clairvoyant was being a *real* psychic.

Because if something came naturally to her, it couldn't be that great, now could it?

Daniel shook his head at Ruby and opened his mouth to reply when a portly waiter arrived, carrying a tray with four huge bowls of steaming soup on it. A slender woman followed with a second tray holding small plates filled with basil leaves, bean sprouts, and bottles of what were clearly house-made hot sauce.

The soup smelled amazing. Chicken, scallions, and a hint of ginger. When one of the big, white bowls was set in front of her, Tempest couldn't help but lean forward and inhale.

Daniel tasted his soup, then grabbed a hot sauce and squirted some in. Tempest tentatively took a basil sprig and began tearing leaves, watching them drop onto the surface of the soup.

Ruby scissored up a pile of bean sprouts with the bright green chopsticks that arrived with the food and grinned at her. Tempest smiled back, then ducked her head back to her soup.

"The guy isn't anyone I recognize, but dudes like him are everywhere," Daniel said. "Probably some libertarian daddy's boy or something. We squash one set of them, and another set pops up."

"They do resemble roaches," Lawrence said. "Eventually we'll find the thing that gets rid of them, once and for all."

Tempest hoped so. Arrow and Crescent had more than one run in with right wingers, and her vision from earlier, coupled with Ruby's description of the man, made her skin crawl. She shook it off and dipped a ceramic spoon into the soup. Before it reached her lips, she heard her name.

It was Lawrence again. "You good, Tempest? You look a little pale. I mean, paler than usual."

She felt her face flush and cleared her throat. She turned. She could focus on Lawrence next to her, and not on Daniel and Ruby across the table.

"I had a vision this afternoon."

She felt Lawrence go still inside. Felt it with her body. Her clairsentience again. "What kind of vision?"

Daniel slurped at his soup. Tempest cheated a glance his way, only to see Ruby hit his ribs with an elbow.

"Ouch! What was that for?"

"Pay attention, doofus!"

"I am!"

Lawrence glared at both of them.

"Go on," he said.

Tempest just wanted to fade into the background and eat her soup. For one thing, the soup was really good. Secondly, while she didn't have social anxiety, she was shy enough around strangers that she just needed more time to acclimate. Selene said she needed to work on calibrating her energy fields so other people's energy didn't affect her so much.

At any rate, she wasn't there yet. Lawrence was cool. She knew him. Daniel, she'd met before. Ruby? Not only was she new, she was super hot, and her energy field was huge.

"Tempest?" Lawrence asked.

She shoved the bowl away a few inches and tucked her chin into her hands. Find time. Buying time.

"I had a vision," she finally said. "And I think it was that guy. At least, your description sounds like what he looks like. And I got the same feeling when you described him as I did in the vision."

"I'm not sure what you mean," Ruby said, her forehead furrowed.

Oh, just great, now she would know that Tempest was a freak. Not that Tempest would ever pluck up the courage to date someone as bright and shiny as Ruby in the first place. But a girl could still dream, couldn't she?

Tempest looked at Lawrence, asking for help.

He leaned into the table, shrinking the distance between the two sides, and lowered his voice. "Let's try this," he said. "People, places, objects, they all have signatures that we recognize. You get a different feeling in this restaurant, for example, then you do it Cider Liberation, or the hotel we were just at, right?"

Ruby nodded.

"Well, it's the same with dreams or visions," he said. "Everything in a dream or vision makes you feel a certain way. That's its energetic signature. So, believe in magic or not, that stuff exists."

"Okay, I can go with that," Ruby said. "I think I understand."

Ruby and Lawrence both turn to look at her, while Daniel slurped his soup. Tempest took a deep breath, and tried to find the words, hidden somewhere in the maze of her fluttering belly and discordant mind. If she was going to be a witch, she had to find her power, at least that's what Raquel and Brenda were always saying.

"So, he felt like the guy you're describing. Down to the reverse pentagram and the way he made your skin crawl, and the hair stand up on the back of your neck."

"What was he doing in your vision?" Lawrence asked. "Did you get a sense of what he wanted?"

Tempest cupped her hands around the warm basin of soup, pulling it back toward her, trying to stave off the chill building in her core.

She looked Lawrence dead in the eyes. He stared right back. Waiting.

"For some reason, I think he's going after Arrow and Crescent. And it feels really bad."

Lawrence sat back in booth, with a huffed exhalation.

"Well, holy shit," he said.

Tempest had to agree.

10

RUBY

Ruby padded around her workroom in her socks, digging through bins, searching out replacement stock to bring to Geeks and Bells in the morning. She should probably be sleeping, all things considered, but was too keyed up after dinner, and had invited Daniel back to her place for a drink.

Daniel swiveled in the deep green 1950s chair Ruby lounged in when she needed a break. In one hand, he held a can of hard seltzer, while the other tugged on the short, jet black spikes of his hair. The chair sat in an ell created by two of the three cubby shelf units that lined the walls of the room. Her loom took up one half of the floor space, with a spinning wheel and the comfy chair and floor lamp the other.

Some hip-hop punk rhymes were on low, barely competing with a cat yowling outside. Portland local Ivan was rapping about art and carcinogens but Ruby wasn't in the mood. She needed something softer in order to think. Punk, rap, and metal were good for cutting loose, or for working, but not for thinking.

She clicked through her phone, finally settling on piano covers of the Pixies. Now who was old? Ruby sighed.

She really wanted more time with Tempest, but the woman had looked so startled when Ruby had entered her digits into her phone, she figured that was going to take some time. If it happened at all.

Ball was in Tempest's court, and Ruby knew better than to push someone as shy as that.

She rooted through bins in yet another cubby unit on the third wall. The fourth wall was hung with a weaving she'd been gifted with a few years before. It was a spectacular piece, shot through with crimson, turquoise, rust, and green. Broad black stripes bordered the edges. Ruby had started out on her weaving stool, and a can of mildly alcoholic grapefruit seltzer water sat waiting for her on the small side table near Daniel, but her body needed to move. She needed to be busy.

"I don't get it," she said, then pulled out a set of long scarves woven in Angry Birds colors. Not as popular as a few years ago, the primary colors still sold just fine, and when it came to making her holiday nut, that would do.

"Don't get what?"

"This Satanist dude, or whatever he is."

"What about him don't you get?"

Ruby snapped the lid back on the tote bin and slid it back onto the shelf. She turned, scarves in hand. The texture felt good on her fingers. She liked things to be tangible. Real.

"I don't know. Everything. And all this magic stuff. It's just...weird."

Daniel cracked a grin at that and took a sip from his can.

Ruby put the scarves in the "go to the event" bin and flopped back down on the weaving stool, picking up her own can of grapefruit seltzer. The bracing beverage was better in the summer, when it was hot out, but it was what was in the fridge, bought by Ruby's housemates in late September and languishing since.

Speaking of housemates, Desi and Mark erupted into laughter in the next room. Sounded like they were watching a video. The two of them loved movie night in bed. She teased them about being old, even though they were her age. They were great people to live with, paid rent on time and kept the common spaces clean, and that was all that mattered. They didn't need to be best friends.

"What do you want to know about magic? I only dabble in it, myself, so you might be better off with Lawrence...or Tempest." He added that last with another wicked grin.

"Shut up."

He returned to swiveling in her chair and drinking seltzer. One thing she liked about Daniel: he was content to wait out her silences. That was one reason she liked hanging out with him. Not that she didn't love her queer and lesbian crew, but they wanted to process more than she was willing to. It eventually strained a relationship, that tension between oversharing to death and not sharing quite enough.

The soothing music filled the room.

"I'm trying to figure out what questions I even have," Ruby said. "I mean, the only Satanists I know are you and your friends, and the only witches I've met before have been a little too loopy for my tastes, you know?"

Daniel, left foot on right knee, leaned forward in the chair, overbalancing a bit. He caught the chair in mid-swivel and smacked both stockinged feet onto the wood floor. He groused about having to unlace his boots every fucking time he visited, but he did it anyway. With him, the complaining was pro forma. Ruby respected it.

Besides, she knew Daniel's parents would have his hide if he ever set foot in their home with his shoes on.

"You have to just think of them as another class of nerd. Witches, magicians, and even the non-theist Satanists of my group? They're not that different from RPG crews, LARPers, or Trekkies. They've got their own symbol systems. Their own stories and myths. Their own beliefs of right and wrong. And they can be just as passionately geeky about it all or lean more toward the norm end of the spectrum."

"Huh." Ruby didn't know what to say to that, so she took another swallow of grapefruit seltzer. "So how is this Satanist dude different from ASP?"

Setting her can on a side table, she pulled her favorite wood drop spindle out of an old metal whiskey canister, then reached for a hank of undyed wool. Made of walnut, the spindle looked like a cross between old fashioned wood top and a child's play sword. She wound the piece of leader yarn around the wooden shaft before looping it through the hook at the top of the round whorl. Then, grabbing a tuft of wool, she let her body settle into the soothing rhythm of turning carded wool into yarn.

"Well, for starters, he's a fascist, right? And if Tempest's vision turns out to have any truth in it? Sounds like he works actual magic, which could be a problem." Now it was Daniel's turn to sigh. He ran a hand through his hair and leaned back in the chair again, staring at the ceiling.

"Left Hand Path stuff is tricky," he went on. "The folks who are serious about that kind of magic generally come in two camps."

"And those are?"

"On one hand, you have people who believe that to affect real change, we have to include the whole human experience, face our demons, work through our shit, and learn to embrace and integrate every part of our nature. They're often Luciferians. Or some Thelemites."

He grew silent, eyes tracing one large crack in the golden yellow plaster above their heads.

Ruby waited. As she wound the wool onto the spindle and worked the yarn between her fingers, she felt the tension in the room increase. The silence didn't feel companionable anymore, but she didn't want to break into Daniel's thoughts just yet. It felt as if he were knitting something together, and it just might be important.

He tilted his head down, eyes catching on the movement of the drop spindle. He spoke as if the words were being pulled from his mouth, the way Ruby tugged at the wool.

"And on the other hand, the magic can get twisted. Not twisted like that yarn. Snarled. Knotted."

The wool snagged in Ruby's fingers. She cursed under her breath and smoothed it out again. Daniel blinked, but held his eyes steady on her hands. On the spooling out of wool to yarn.

"Those people think magic is all about personal power. Personal liberation. They forget that liberation is never singular. It's always plural."

"What?" The word escaped Ruby's mouth before she could stop it.

Daniel ripped his eyes from her spinning and stared at her, still halfway somewhere else.

"Freedom is a two-edged sword of which one edge is liberty and the other responsibility, on which both edges are exceedingly sharp; and which is not easily handled by casual, cowardly, or treacherous hands." It was clear he was quoting something.

"What's that from?"

"Jack Whiteside Parsons. He was a rocket scientist and a

magician." Daniel shook himself out of his reverie. "He died of an explosion in his lab. Fulminate of mercury. But that's the thing these people don't get. They forget the responsibility part. They think their personal will is the only thing in the world that matters, and that everyone and everything should bow to that."

"That's fucked."

"Tell me about it. At any rate, if this guy is styling himself as a Satanist, and actually working some sort of magic? Odds are good he's exactly that type of self-centered asshole, which pisses me off. Not only is it dangerous, it gives Satanism a bad name."

Ruby stopped her spindle and burst out laughing. Daniel looked startled.

"What?"

"You actually. Just said. 'Gives Satanism a bad name.'"

Daniel grinned, then started laughing himself.

The heavy tension in the room broke. Ruby rocked and laughed, throttling it back long enough to take a drink. Daniel did the same.

Then they both started laughing again. It felt so good, to laugh that way.

Finally, the mania subsided. Daniel crushed his empty can in his hands.

"The question is, what are we gonna do about this guy? I'll need to check in with ASP. They hate this sort of shit. And it's not as if we don't already have enough issues to deal with in this city, right?"

Ruby shook her head. "That's the truth."

She bundled the wool back into a bag and wound the yarn onto the spindle before setting it next to the drop spindle on the small table.

"You'll let me know what I can do to help? I mean, I don't

know shit about magic and all that, but if this jerk is gunning for your crew, or targeting anarchist witches on my watch? I'm down to do something about it."

Daniel nodded. "Sure thing. And remember, you could just think of it as a big LARP. Got any more of this?"

He shook the empty can.

"That I do."

As she headed for the kitchen to fetch another can of hard seltzer, she pondered what Daniel had just said.

Maybe she *could* just think of the woo stuff as live action role play. She could temporarily suspend her disbelief, and just get through whatever this weirdness was in one piece.

11

TEMPEST

Steam from the tub swirled around her. It wasn't the claw foot tub Tempest wanted, but for an apartment above a garage to have a tub at all was pretty great. Graymalkin stared at her with his big orange kitty eyes from his perch on the tub's edge. FKA twigs played from her phone on the small sink vanity. Twigs' ethereal voice had captured Tempest from the first time she heard her booming from a car during her sophomore year. That school year had felt particularly shitty and listening to twigs made her feel as if she could float away from it all.

The way she was doing now.

The garage apartment belonged to Selene's boyfriend, Joshua. He'd let her paint it the way she wanted, and the pale blue walls of the bathroom were one result. As was evidenced around the small apartment, that even though she wore a lot of black and yellow, Tempest also liked pretty much every shade of blue. The color calmed her. She sank deeper into the bath, until the hot water scented with lavender and rose was all the way up to her chin. Then she closed her eyes.

Home. This apartment, and this bathtub, were another place that finally felt like home.

But now home was threatened. The careful equilibrium Tempest had built with the coven, with the shop, and with working her ass off to train as a massage therapist...whoever this guy was? He was definitely gunning for it all.

Oh, his sights weren't trained on her, specifically. But bad magic aimed at the coven itself? That may as well be a direct threat. And the fact that he'd also shown up to harass Ruby? A person Tempest might actually be interested in?

"What kind of coincidence is that?"

A bad one. The worst. She glanced at her phone, remembering the way Ruby had laughed. The woman had stared at her with deep black eyes set in that gorgeous, round face, and asked her point blank to unlock it.

"Why?" Tempest had stupidly replied. Gah. She felt like such an idiot, just thinking about it.

That was when Ruby had laughed and said, "Because I want to give you my phone number. Isn't it obvious?"

As if beautiful women gave Tempest their phone numbers all the time. As if Tempest was someone who could be noticed. Seen.

Tempest let the music carry her. And the memory of Ruby's lips. The wide, smiling lips the same color as her name. Something in Tempest uncoiled at the memory and she realized she wanted Ruby. Like, her body wanted her.

"It's just the music, stupid." Twigs' voice. Singing about the kind of sex that only kinky angels must have.

But it wasn't just twigs. And she knew it. Tempest exhaled, and slid her hands across her belly, moving down.

Her phone began to buzz, interrupting the music. Jittering across the vanity countertop, it danced toward the edge.

"Shit!"

Tempest pushed up from the tub, swiped her hands across a towel, reached, and grabbed. Graymalkin leapt with an annoyed squeak and stalked out the door.

Tempest caught the phone right before it slipped over the edge. Thank Diana her bathroom was small.

It was Raquel. Raquel never called. Always texted if she needed anything.

Tempest stepped onto the bathmat, water streaming down her body, and grabbed a towel before answering. Damn it. There was going to be water everywhere.

"Raquel?"

The older woman's voice was on edge. Tempest's heart raced.

"No. I'm fine. Are you sure?"

Tempest wrapped the towel around her skinny frame.

"I...Brenda told you about the vision?"

Graymalkin, who had paused just outside the bathroom door to groom water from his fur, blinked his orange eyes at her.

"Yeah. I'll be careful. Okay. Yes. I'll boost my wards tonight. Yes. Talk tomorrow. Thanks. Yeah. Blessed be."

Tempest stared back at Graymalkin. "Raquel had a vision, too. Someone attacking a witch. We'd better get to work."

She would boost her wards, all right. And then she was going to pull some cards.

Tempest finished toweling off, then dropped the towel on the floor to soak up some of the water and turned to pull the plug on the tub. As the fragrant water gurgled from the tub, Tempest stepped past Graymalkin, headed to the battered pine dresser she'd painted a deep teal blue, and grabbed her striped flannel pajamas. Luckily, Arrow and

Crescent coven believed a witch could do magic anywhere, anytime, and wearing anything or nothing.

"Okay, Graymalkin. What do you think?"

The cat didn't respond, but instead of curling up on his favorite burgundy floor cushion, remained alert, still looking at her with those inscrutable, orange eyes.

Tempest stood in the center of the open room. Tiny kitchen to her left. Bed to her right. Comfy brown chair with matching ottoman angled near the bookcases set beneath the window in front of her, facing east. A loveseat Joshua and Selene had helped her rescue from the street. She'd gotten a blue slipcover for it, making it look almost new. Heavy navy curtains were drawn to block out the winter night and the streetlamp she knew would be shining through the bare elm branches in front of the neighbor's house across the street.

Her altar space was on top of the bookcases. Simple. Like this apartment, the altar was just the right amount of space for what she needed.

The only light in the room came from the floor lamp near the chair and one of the twin lamps set on the small nightstands that graced either side of her bed.

"Tools, or no tools?" That was one thing about living with an animal, Tempest had discovered. She talked out loud more these days.

Phone back in hand, she cast her attention outward, seeking. Trying to assess her home space, and what was just beyond her space. Other than a hairline crack in the southwest, her apartment wards felt fine. Her attention flowed further. Joshua's house wards. They seemed strong. Good. and the property...?

Well, shit. There it was, in the southwest again. A fissure the size of an apple at the heart of it, radiating outward, thinner and thinner, feeling like concrete that had been smacked one too many times with a sledge.

She texted Joshua. Selene would probably be talking to him about it, but just in case.

Breach in the southwest property wards. Small crack in my apartment protection. Your house seems fine.

Three floating dots indicated that he was typing.

Well, shit. Was just about to check. Selene told me. I'm on it. Need anything?

Tempest scanned her space again. Nothing seemed amiss. Nothing in the space that shouldn't be there. That was good.

Doesn't feel like anything got in. I'll repair the crack here.

Joshua texted back a thumbs-up.

She threw her phone on the bed. No tools, then. Keep it simple. Just the body and breath of the witch.

Graymalkin stalked over and sat. Looking up at her, he meowed.

"Thanks, buddy. Can you anchor me?"

He yawned, showing pink gums and sharp fangs, then curled up on her toes.

Tempest smiled. Whether Graymalkin was just a plain old cat, an emotional service animal, or a familiar, it didn't matter. He always knew when she needed something, and usually complied, even if he sometimes put up a fuss about it. And if he felt she might be a little off balance? Onto her feet or her lap it was.

She let the feel of his soft gray fur on her skin bring her spirit all the way back into her body. Another thing to work on: when she got scared or nervous, part of her wanted to escape. That was a result of not feeling safe as a child, Brenda had said. Graymalkin sure did help.

Tempest slowed her breathing way down, concentrating

on opening her feet and breathing as deeply into her belly as possible, before allowing the air to rise up into her chest.

Reaching deep, she called up the red-hot fire at the heart of the earth, and felt it pool up through her feet, rising to her belly. Reaching up, she called down the white coolness of the moon, feeling it cascade down through her, mixing with the earth fire. This helped orient her to the magic. The sense of it came winging to her, surrounding her edges, bringing the scent of night-time winter air. The snap of cold. The tang of woodsmoke.

"By earth, by flame, by wind, by sea..." The opening of the circle-casting cantrip centered her more deeply, orienting herself to the magic. The tingle of magic gathered around her, joining with the energy she called into her body.

"By moon, by sun, by dusk, by dark..."

She let her breath and energy fill the sphere of her aura, and breathed outward, matching the shape of her aura with the sphere that surrounded her home.

The power of earth and sky, of the coming Solstice, of the winter's night, and her own, personal magic all coiled together, increasing in power on every breath. Finally, it was ready. Tempest held out her hands and felt the energy flow from her fingers, outward, toward her wards.

"By witch's mark!" She said the words with force, and gave a mighty push. The edges of her skin flared, and in her mind's eye, she imagined the sphere around her small apartment flare at the same time.

Palms up, she stood in the center of her studio apartment and breathed, the exhilaration of the magic still within her.

Graymalkin uncoiled himself from her feet and walked back to his cushion.

Tempest smiled.

"Take that, asshole. We're on to you."

Whoever the asshole was, and whatever his issue was, the coven was ready.

And Tempest was, too.

At least, she hoped so.

12

RUBY

The only other living things around were a flock of robins, racing through bare branches and alighting to feast on desiccated lawns. That, and a cat, glaring at her from a half dark porch. Frost glowed ghostly on lawns and the evergreens.

The air iced her cheeks, and she tugged her navy watch cap down over her ears.

The cadence of Ruby's sneakers on the sidewalk blended with the song piped through her earbuds. It was some ambient funk she hoped would ease her into the day. It was seven thirty on a Sunday morning, and in the gray, pre-dawn light, it felt as though the forecast snow just might be on the way.

She flipped her hood over the watch cap. Even with the long underwear beneath her workout gear, jogging in the cold wasn't her favorite, but if you didn't exercise in Portland because of weather, you wouldn't exercise all winter, and huge chunks of spring and fall. And Ruby needed the run to clear her head and get ready for her busy day. She'd stayed up way too late last night, talking with Daniel, and dreaming about Tempest.

Plus, she was worried the asshole was going to show up at Geeks and Bells again. That was the last thing she needed. Besides, if she didn't make enough money this weekend, it meant her business was officially in trouble. While yesterday's sales had been more than decent, summer had been slower than usual. The autumn fairs had brought in money, but not quite enough to see her through until things picked up again.

She'd given herself three years to squeak by and try to make a go of it, but business was hard. It wasn't her work ethic that was the problem, it was the ups and downs of sales. Maybe she needed to join that small artist's mastermind a local Pagan jeweler had invited her to. But anything called "mastermind" gave Ruby hives. And, while she had no issue with Pagans, why did it suddenly seem she was surrounded?

Weird.

But it was either join a mastermind and really figure the business stuff out or get a job with that receptionist agency that let people wear what they wanted because they weren't going to workspaces on site. It seemed like a cool company, but Ruby...

She really wanted to make it on her own. Getting a second job felt like defeat. Oh, her friends all insisted that wasn't true, and a lot of them did the whole side hustle thing. But she didn't want a side hustle. She wanted a career.

A car cruised by, either someone heading home after a night out, or some poor sucker who had to work at eight o'clock on a Sunday morning.

"Pick up the pace, Rubes." If she didn't get a different kind of hustle on, she wouldn't have time for breakfast before heading to the hotel. And to face a room full of geeks, bouncing off the walls? Even if they were some of her favorite people, Ruby needed to be well fortified.

She had to get through the geek craft fair, load her stuff up, and have drinks with Sean and Carla, hopefully all of it Nazi free.

But she couldn't help thinking of a small woman with platinum-blond hair. She really hoped Tempest would text.

But like all things in life, Ruby wasn't going to count on it. You made your own luck, she believed, and other people did, too. That meant sometimes your luck got cancelled out. Life was a crap shoot sometimes, but at least that kept things interesting.

13

TEMPEST

Tempest stood in her micro kitchen, which consisted of a mini fridge, two-burner cook top, a microwave, kettle, sink, and some cherry-stained cabinets. She'd put up a peel-and-stick backsplash of black and white tiles in a Moroccan pattern and was pretty pleased with the result.

Still in her pajamas, she waited for the small electric kettle to boil. Her feet were bare, and the wood floor was cold. She alternated propping her feet one on top of the other. That only succeeded in making the tops of her feet as cold as the bottoms. She had perfectly good slippers her coven mate Alejandro had given her last Yule, plus a drawer filled with cozy socks, but until she got some tea into her this morning? She didn't have the gumption to walk back across the studio to get either.

That's the way it was sometimes.

The power of last night's magic had faded, leaving Tempest feeling cold and uncertain again. Magic was like that. At least for her. The energy puffed her up, made her feel larger and more powerful than she actually was, then, as the energetic tide went out, left her feeling smaller than before.

She was supposed to be working on that. Both Brenda and Raquel told her that the magic was trying to show her the power that was already inside her. It lay dormant, the way some seeds were dormant, waiting for the magic of the sun to warm the soil. She caught the sense of it when they were talking, but as soon as she was on her own again, the feeling was gone.

She just didn't believe it.

So, use your imagination, dummy.

Yeah. Easier said than done.

Graymalkin was still curled up on the bed, and Tempest felt very tempted to join him. Winter was always hard, which reminded her, she really needed to take her Vitamin D. She grabbed a brown glass bottle from the counter and popped a small pill beneath her tongue and sighed. She should also meditate in front of her light box every morning. As a matter of fact, she should do all the things that were supposed to help her energy levels, and she would, as soon as she had a cup of tea.

Morning practice—which was required for all coven members—was really hard during the cold and dark. She could almost hear Brenda saying, "When it's hardest is when you need it most."

Still easier said than done.

The kettle finally clicked off, steam pouring from the spout.

"Thank Diana!" she said, plopping an English Breakfast bag into her favorite Orca mug and pouring the steaming water over it, watching the brown of the tea leach into clear water. That done, she grabbed a carton of oat milk and waited for the tea to brew. Her feet were impersonating ice blocks by this point, so she hurried across the hardwood floors to grab the blue wool slippers from where she'd kicked them at the foot of the bed.

It was a weird thing. She was used to taking care of her basic needs after years of self-sufficiency, but she still wasn't used to taking care of anything beyond that. She always had rent and phone money, and enough for food, but the rest of it? Meh. Anything beyond pure survival just slipped off her radar. The coven had been working on her, but she had to choose to take care of herself.

She knew that.

Just like she was coming to know that it was normal to have conflicting desires. Everyone had that, apparently, which had been news to her. Her desire to hole up and be left alone to be as small as she felt was always going to be at war with her desire to feel the way she felt when she did magic. Or when she was around the coven. Powerful. Strong. Not invincible, but centered and certain.

She felt freer then, too. More like the person she wanted to be. Not the doofus who blushed and stammered around beautiful women.

Her feet were feeling better but now the rest of her was cold. She pulled a hoodie on over her pajamas, scratched Graymalkin's head, and went to doctor up her tea.

She couldn't stand around all morning, thinking of all the ways she didn't measure up. She had a shift at the Inner Eye today, and a new massage client to email back before heading in to work.

Frankly, it would be good to get out, do something. See people other than her cat. And talk about something other than the thoughts that kept swirling in her mind.

All the same, she couldn't help but feel something was really wrong with her. And that her coven mates were just being kind to say she was as normal as any other human weirdo they knew.

Today? Tempest felt like the Tarot card, the five of discs. Always on the outside of the building, struggling along in the cold and snow, wishing she could feel the warm lights that glowed inside.

Some days it felt as if everyone could feel the warmth but her. Maybe her last foster mom was right, and Tempest was somehow broken inside.

14

RUBY

Other than some quiet voices and the occasional laugh, the vast hotel ballroom was quiet. Lights hummed and the orange and brown carpets clashed with pretty much everything. That didn't matter. All eyes would be trained above, and the carpets covered by an endless flow of sneakers, boots, and wheelchairs.

Ruby loved the calm before the hordes arrived, when it was just vendors in their booths, making last-minute adjustments to their wares and drinking coffee. It spoke of possibility. And after yesterday's weirdness, it was good to be back to that.

Ruby stepped outside her booth and looked at it from across the aisle. It looked great, she decided. Her two tables looked full. Wooden dowel racks stood near the backs of the tables, soft, brightly woven scarves and shawls hanging on display. Her cash point tablet was tucked discreetly into a back corner, along with a locking metal cash box buried beneath gift bags on a low shelving unit behind a padded folding stool. She tried to not perch on that too much, but it was necessary for those moments when she just had to get off her boots for a few minutes.

The stock she'd lugged in this morning had filled in the gaps made by yesterday's sales. With her phone charged up and cash box filled with change for the few oldsters that still actually handled filthy lucre, she was as prepared as she could be. That was good, considering the doors opened in three minutes. Just enough time to pour herself a cup of cardamom coffee from the thermos she had filled at home.

She smelled Bay Rum and felt the air shift right before she turned.

"Good morning!" Sean suddenly towered over her, shaggy blond hair wet combed from his morning shower. For such a mountain of a man, he sure was a soft walker. Today's uniform was a Timbers Army T-shirt—along with being toy makers and geeks, Sean and Carla were serious soccer fans—black jeans, and green Pumas.

"Good morning yourself. Ready for the day?"

"Yep." He crossed large, tattooed arms over his chest and rocked back and forth on his heels. "Just wanted to let you know that I heard from security. They talked with the guy but since he didn't steal anything or assault anyone, there's nothing they can do."

"Can't kick someone out because of their thoughts, right? I mean, I get it, but it's still frustrating. How many people have to get beaten up or killed by these goons before we can preempt them?"

The sound of the laughs and chatter filtered into the big ballroom. Doors must be open.

Sean sighed and shrugged. "We just have to back each other up. I gotta get to the booth. See you after load out."

"Thanks, Sean. See you."

And then the day got busy. Ruby was in her element. Helping people try on shawls, picking out the perfect scarf or hatband for gifts, selling more woven bracelets and bookmarks.

But the back of her mind still nagged at her. Something was still wrong. That guy wasn't gone. She just knew it.

"Hey, lady?" A little voice came from behind her.

Ruby turned and smiled down at a small Asian boy wearing a Miles Morales Spider-Man T-shirt. He looked to be around nine.

"Hi there! What's your name?"

"Charles."

"What can I help you with, Charles?"

He held out a fisted hand. "I found this."

An amulet rested in his palm. Ruby bit back a curse.

It was a pewter Black Sun. A solar disc comprised of a circle with the sharp, slashed shapes of the runes for the sun forming a ring of rays around it. Talking with folks like Daniel, Ruby knew the original came from tile work in Heinrich Himmler's castle.

These days, it was only used by serious neo-Nazis and certain occultists. Like the kind of Satanist skinny guy was turning out to be.

She forced herself to keep smiling and remain calm. With a quick glance around, she saw her booth customers all seemed happily occupied, so she crouched down next to Charles and held out her hand, willing herself not to snatch the amulet from his precious little palm.

"Someone must have dropped it," she said. "If you give it to me, I can keep it in the booth in case they come back. And I can tell Lost and Found I have it."

"Okay," he said, and plunked the cast pewter in her hand. "Do you have any Spider-Man scarfs?"

Ruby exhaled, smiled again, and stood.

"I sure do. At least I have Spider-Man colors. All the scarves are over here. I've got super long ones, and shorter ones that might fit you better."

"Oh, it's not for me!" he said, gravely. "It's for my Grandpa. He loves Spider-Man as much as I do."

This time, Ruby's smile was genuine. "Let's go find him one. Do you have an adult around?"

Charles nodded and pointed toward Sean and Carla's booth. "There's my parents."

Sure enough, a man and woman that looked like a couple were there, picking out toys. The woman smiled and waved. Charles and Ruby waved back.

Then she slipped the amulet into the pocket of her jeans. It felt as if it left an oily residue on her fingers, and she immediately regretted putting into her pocket. But she'd deal with that once Charles was sorted out.

He was already at the rack of scarves set up in the back corner of her booth, carefully lifting first one, and then the other.

Ruby greeted an earnest white woman around her age in black framed glasses and black cat ears. The woman nodded, mumbled out an "I'm fine. Just looking," and bent her head back to the infinity loop neck warmers. Cute, but shy. The neck warmers were knitted by Ruby's friend, Grace. She'd taken them on consignment just for this show, and so far, they were doing pretty well.

Okay. Charles.

"Did you find the Spider-Man scarves?"

She really loved the red, blue, and black scarves. The simple pattern was a satisfying weave and the colors looked great. The fact that she could sell them to geeks and then to regular people at the more standard craft fairs was a plus.

His brow furrowed. "I did. But how can you tell they're for Spider-Man and not Superman?"

She smiled. Kids were so awesome. Reaching up, she pulled down a red and blue scarf with a white border. This style had a particularly tight weave and felt smooth to the touch.

"Superman's has white, see? Spider-Man's has black, for the spider."

Charles's face cleared. "Oh. Duh! Thanks! Let me go get my mom and dad! They said if I picked out Grandpa's present, they'd pay."

"Good deal. See you soon."

She watched him run to his parents, who'd moved on to the booth across from Ruby's. He gesticulated with excitement.

Other than Cat Girl—who was still absorbed, holding up scarf after scarf—for the moment, the booth was clear.

Time to get the damn amulet out of her pocket.

Ruby stepped behind the table that held her cash point tablet and the cash box buried beneath a pile of festive paper bags with handles and her business info and logo stamped on the front.

Where should she put it? Not in the cash box, that was for sure.

She grabbed a piece of red tissue paper and pulled the thing out. A rough edge caught her right pointer finger, nicking her.

"Damn!" Her finger flew to her mouth. As soon as she sucked on the small wound, she wondered if it was a mistake.

What? You think the amulet is full of nasty magic or something? Come on, Rubes.

What did she think this was? A D&D quest? The third

level of Skyrim? Despite last night's conversation, the whole thing still felt...weird. Even though she took Daniel's point, she'd always been quite happy to keep the line between gaming and real life quite firm. Clearly she was straddling some weird in-between state.

Besides, she trusted Daniel and Lawrence. Neither of them were flakes.

And Tempest, she thought. *Maybe you're willing to suspend some disbelief on her account.*

That was probably true. And wasn't it a damn thing? To have avoided falling for someone in so long, only to have a shy witch invade her mind?

Two Black men—one in a Shazam T-shirt and the other wearing a blue Starfleet hoodie—walked into the booth, smiled, and headed toward her.

"Hey!" Shazam asked. "Got anything for kids?"

"I sure do," Ruby replied, pasting her craft fair smile back on her face. She shoved the amulet back into her pocket. She'd deal with it later. Maybe call Daniel. See what he thought.

For now, though? These two men needed help and it looked as if Cat Girl might be ready to actually buy something.

"Be right with you!" she said.

Ruby gave the clear plastic bottle on her table a pump and rubbed disinfectant all over her hands, paying special attention to the nicked finger.

It stung.

15

TEMPEST

It was still early enough that the post-brunch Sunday crowd hadn't yet hit the store. Lawrence had stopped by for a chat and leaned against the glass counter as Tempest made up some inexpensive necklaces for display. Her small fingers were perfect for untangling things, and the results were two neat piles of burgundy and deep blue silk cords laid out on the glass countertop, ready for pendants and charms.

"I don't know, Lawrence. I'm pretty sure it's just me, freaking out. You know I'm not really clairvoyant and, I mean, what are the odds?"

"What's it gonna take, Tempest? Do you need an actual Nazi to walk through your front door?"

The bells on the Inner Eye door chimed. Tempest's head snapped up, heart racing. She huffed out an exhalation and felt her shoulders drop when she saw who it was. Cassiel.

A riot of red curls peaked out from beneath a green wool cap. A matching scarf wound around the woman's neck, covering her up to her chin.

"Cassie! What are you doing here? Don't you work today?"

Her coven mate smiled and held out a brown cardboard tray filled with white paper cups. "Nope. I get Sundays off now, and I brought hot chocolate! I know Brenda has tea and all, but it's cold out today, and a little birdie told me you might need some cheering up."

The bells chimed again as Cassie was still talking. Everyone turned to the newcomer, swathed in a black wool coat and boots along with a white scarf and soft wool hat. Dark hair framed her boss's smiling face. Brenda was here, and everything felt slightly better.

"Who needs cheering up?" Brenda asked, unwinding the scarf and unbuttoning her coat. "And do I smell chocolate?"

Cassiel set the takeout tray on the counter and slipped off her gloves and hat, shoving both into the pocket of her own black coat. Even the witches who loved color seemed to wear a lot of black.

"Cassie seems to think I do," Tempest said, watching her mentor head toward the purple, Celtic knot work curtain that separated the shop from the meeting room-slash-break room.

"I brought hot chocolate for everyone."

"Just let me hang my coat up and I'll be back. Cassie, need me to take your coat?"

Smiling, Cassie handed her things to Brenda, who swished through the curtain and disappeared.

"Wait." Lawrence was staring at the white cups. "There's four cups. How'd you know I was going to be here?"

Cassie looked at Tempest and they both laughed.

"How do you think?" Cassiel replied.

"Witches." Lawrence shook his head and *tsked*.

"I don't think you're one to talk, Lawrence," Brenda said,

adjusting the knot of loose dark waves at the top of her head. She looked splendid, as always, in a thigh-length teal blue sweater tunic, black leggings, and boots. Silver bracelets, silver earring dangles, and a silver necklace set with a large moonstone completed her "hot, middle-aged psychic and Witch" look.

Brenda always seemed so composed and, well, together. Tempest wished some of that would rub off. She always felt half stuck together, as if a manic Faery Goddess had a field day with sticks and glue.

Tempest popped the lid off her cup and sniffed the rich scents of chocolate, cinnamon, and warm oat milk.

"Thanks, Cassie. But I still don't see why you thought I needed something."

Lawrence *tsked* again but didn't say anything, too busy sipping his own hot chocolate. The boy sure loved his sweets.

"Frankly, Tempest, you've felt a little haunted lately. And it's not just your health. And then Brenda told me about your vision and...well, let's just say the ghosts were talking and I got a pretty clear message during this morning's meditation."

"And that was?" Brenda asked. She poured her hot chocolate into a blue ceramic mug from the back room. Somehow, she managed to pull it off without hot liquid cascading all over the countertop. One long, beringed finger caught an errant drop before it slid off the side of the cup. Brenda hated drinking out of anything other than glass or ceramic if she could help it.

Everyone had their quirks.

Tempest concentrated on drinking her own hot chocolate, hoping a customer would walk through the door, which would mean she or Brenda would need to help them, and would mean whatever Cassiel had come in to tell her could wait.

Maybe forever. It was bad enough having Lawrence on her case, and the visions, and everything else going on, without getting confirmation that things were about to get more real than she had the capacity to handle.

"Tempest?" Brenda looked at her with concern. "You've just gotten even paler than you were five seconds ago. What's going on?"

"I just..." How could she explain it? She wasn't even certain why she was struggling like this. Confirmation that she wasn't just losing her mind would be good, right?

But all of a sudden, everything just felt too big. Too dangerous. Too real.

"She's scared," Lawrence finally said. "And she doesn't want to admit that shit is about to go down. Again. There's stuff you don't know yet..."

"Lawrence." Tempest's voice came out as a whisper, hardly a threat, but Lawrence stopped anyway, cleared his throat, and took another drink of chocolate.

"Tempest? Can you tell us?" Brenda asked, squeezing her wrist gently before releasing her again.

Tempest shook her head, and stared down at her cup, then at the neat piles of satin cords. She really just wanted an ordinary day at the shop. She just wanted to slide crescent moons and brass pentacles onto those cords and arrange them on the display. Then she wanted to get a slice of pizza with Lawrence. Go back to her apartment. Pet Graymalkin and curl up with the urban fantasy she was reading.

"This weaver we know, Ruby, was vending at a craft fair yesterday and thinks she saw the dude from Tempest's vision."

"I knew it," Cassiel said. "That's what the ghosts were

saying this morning. That the danger was real—closer than we thought—and that Tempest was in the middle of it all."

"But why?" Tempest didn't understand it. None of it. Why her? Why now? "Why me? I mean, I get why someone would be pissed off at the coven, but what have *I* done?"

Brenda looked at her with those wise blue eyes, brimming with compassion, but still seeing way too much for Tempest's comfort.

"Sometimes things don't make sense, Tempest. They just happen. But I don't think that's one-hundred percent the case this time."

Cassie nodded in agreement, red curls swishing around her face.

"You're right, Brenda. As usual. This isn't random. Tempest is being targeted, along with Arrow and Crescent."

"And Daniel has a name now. Brad Chadwick."

"Well," Brenda said, "that's interesting, isn't it? I refused to hire a reader by that name. Joshua did, too."

"Wow," Lawrence said. "That makes it more personal, doesn't it?"

"But why me?" Tempest repeated, voice louder than before. "That's the thing I still don't understand. Why would anyone even notice me?"

A strange look crossed Lawrence's face. Some mix of pity, affection, and disbelief.

"A lot of people notice you, Tempest. You're going to need to get used to it," he said.

Tempest waved him away and turned back to her mentor.

"You're coming into your powers," Brenda said. "And a lot of beings are noticing, for good or ill. Did you up your wards?"

"Yeah. I just did...oh shit."

Her cracked apartment wards, hopefully all repaired now. She had forgotten about them with everything else going on.

That was another thing to tell Cassiel and Brenda. They didn't know about that little attack yet.

The bells chimed. A customer entered the store.

"We aren't done with this conversation," Brenda said, then turned to greet two women who had stopped near the Tarot and pendulum display.

Tempest knew they weren't done. Nothing about whatever this situation turned out to be was done.

And she hated it. All the places that she'd come to know as home—the shop, her apartment, the coven—suddenly didn't feel so safe anymore.

16

———

RUBY

After load out, Sean, Carla, and Ruby decided both food and drink were in order. Ruby texted Daniel to see if he could join them. She really wanted to offload the damn amulet as soon as she could.

The thing she couldn't figure out was why the hell—and when the hell—he'd planted it. Must've been sometime during their messed-up encounter, because why else would he have bothered? The things didn't look cheap, so there had to be some purpose to them, right?

Just like in a D&D campaign, a wizard wouldn't just leave talismans around for no reason. But damn if Ruby could figure out what it was.

She sat across from Sean and Carla in a wooden booth in a dark, comfortable bar that just happened to have excellent food. A bourbon with a giant rock in it rested at her right hand. Sean and Carla had the same.

It being a Sunday evening, the bar was slow. Only two other tables had patrons, though a few people sat at the long, dark wood bar. Some kind of jazz piped softly through the speakers. Jazz wasn't really Ruby's thing, but the melodic piano and trumpet were a nice respite after the noise of Geeks and Bells. And the dim lighting was nice, too, after a day spent in ballroom lights bouncing off plastic comic book sleeves and hideous swirls of hotel carpet.

"To a prosperous year," Carla said, raising her glass. Her frizzy hair was tied back in a rubber band, but still puffed around her head, matching her round cheeks. Gold-framed glasses perched on her button nose. Carla was a middle-aged elf to Sean's blond Santa. They were pretty awesome. Why didn't she hang out with them more often?

"To a prosperous year," Sean and Ruby said, clinking their squat glasses together. The bourbon smelled of caramel and oak and filled her belly with warmth going down. She set the glass back down. No more booze until she got some food in her. Her phone buzzed on the table. Daniel.

On my way. Order me a medium burger with jack cheese?

"Daniel?" Sean asked.

"Yeah. Says he's en route."

The bartender set down two individual-sized cast iron pans filled with sautéed halved Brussels sprouts and bacon. The food smelled like heaven.

"Be right back with your burgers," he said.

"Oh! Can I order another one? Medium. Jack cheese."

"Will do."

They all speared up a sautéed sprout. Wow, they were good. The Station was pretty fancy for bar food. Ruby didn't often shell out for stuff like this, but damn, she appreciated it when it was in front of her. Or in her mouth.

"At least that asshole didn't come back," Carla said. "He sounded like a creep."

"He felt like a creep," Ruby replied, slipping one of the small bacon pieces onto her fork. Yum. "I hope I never have to see him again, but him dropping the amulet in my booth makes me wonder."

She didn't mention that her new crush had some weird vision about the dude. Sean and Carla were open-minded, but frankly, where would she even start with talking about something like that?

She still had almost zero context for real magic, besides knowing that Daniel and Lawrence were as stable as they came. Despite the magic-is-real stuff, they seemed less prone to wild flights of fancy than some of the other geeks she knew.

The burgers arrived, and the smell was mouthwatering. She never ate much during craft fairs and cons. She was usually too busy to do much more than nibble some almonds and take her bathroom breaks.

She slathered spicy mustard onto the toasted bun, and piled up lettuce, tomato, and a couple of rounds of red onion onto the meat. No cheese for her.

"How do you think you did?" Sean asked. Ruby was thankful for the subject change. Get her mind off of this, at least until Daniel showed up. She stacked the top of the bun onto the burger and picked up the whole warm package.

"Sales seemed great. I won't know until I do a final accounting, but business was steady, and people seemed inclined to buy."

"Us, too," Carla said. "We even sold out of a few things, which is great."

"Which means I know what I'll be focusing on come mid-January, after our vacation," Sean said. "Its always nice to have a focus for new production."

Ruby nodded, mouth full of juicy burger. The door to the bar swung open and Daniel stepped inside, letting a blast of frigid air into the warm space. His blue scarf was wrapped half-way around his face, and the hood was up on his insulated black coat. Stomping his boots on the industrial carpet in front of the door, he took his hands from his pockets and swept off his hood. He gave a wave and walked toward the bar to order a drink.

"I've got a lot of weaving to do, that's for sure. I just hope I made enough money to not have to get a second job this spring."

"I hope so, too," Carla said, dabbing at her lips with a napkin. "You know if you ever need to talk business strategy, we're here for you. We've been making our living this way for a long time."

A sense of relief washed through her.

"Wow. That'd be great. I'm actually going to take you up on that."

And then Daniel was beside the booth, setting down a dark pint of what smelled like ale, shucking his coat and hanging it on a hook at the end, on top of Ruby's.

"Hey, Rubes."

"Hey, yourself. You remember Sean and Carla?"

"Of course."

Sean started to rise, burger still in hand, but Daniel waved him back onto the bench, before sliding in next to Ruby, who scooted over to make room.

"Your burger's on the way. You can have some of my sprouts if you want."

Daniel wrinkled his nose. "No thanks. I'll just drink my beer, instead." He tilted his pint glass toward her. "Cheers."

She lifted her bourbon. "Cheers." It didn't burn quite as warm this time, with the food inside her, but it still tasted good. And ratcheted her anxiety down another notch.

"So, what's up? You said there was more about Nazi Boy?"

Ruby set her glass down again and sighed. "Yeah. He left something at my booth, and it's pretty damn nasty."

"Dropped it, or planted it?" Daniel asked.

Ruby shrugged and grabbed the folded gift bag she'd shoved the amulet into after closing out the booth. "You want to look at this now?"

"May as well, before my burger gets here."

She pulled the tissue paper from the bag and unwrapped the first pewter disc, grateful she didn't need to actually touch it. She held the whole thing out to Daniel, who gestured for her to set it on the table in front of him.

He gave a low whistle. "You weren't kidding. That truly is a nasty piece of work. Damn."

"What is it?" Carla asked.

"A Black Sun. Beloved of Nazi occultists. In other words, a truly messed-up, powerful symbol."

Ruby wiped her hands and held up her right pointer finger. "It bit me."

"May I?" Daniel asked. She nodded, and he brought her finger closer, holding it up toward one of the dim lights on the wall behind their booth. "Just a small cut. Did you cleanse it?"

"I slathered it with disinfectant gel, and I've washed my hands a few times since."

He nodded and gave her hand back to her. "Once we're done here, I'll want to look at it properly. See if he tagged you."

"Tagged her?" Sean asked. "What the hell's that mean?"

Here we go, Ruby thought.

"It means," Daniel replied, taking another drink of his beer, "that the bastard may have either encoded the amulet with a tracking device, or a shunt to drain her energy, or any number of nasty pieces of magic."

"Wait," Carla asked, setting her burger down, "people can do that?"

"People can. And do. And it's really messed up."

Ruby pushed the remains of her burger away and picked up her drink, inhaling the caramel fumes as the big ice cube rattled against the edges of the glass. She set it down again.

She remembered the wheat-blond hair on a tall, skinny man at Cider Liberation. The man who had tripped her.

Was it the same person? Had the asshole approached her booth on purpose?

All of a sudden, Ruby felt a little ill.

17

―――――

TEMPEST

Tempest flipped the main shop lights off, leaving only one dim LED light to cast soft illumination on the Inner Eye shop decal in the front window. Her keys rattled as she shot both deadbolts into the metal door casing.

"Damn, it's cold." She flipped the hood up on her insulated jacket and tugged on some fleece gloves. Even though she preferred her vintage leather, there came a time in every Portland winter when the insulated coat was a necessity. It had been pitch black out for hours now, even though it was only seven. If there hadn't still been a restaurant or two open, it might as well have been ten p.m. instead of seven.

Passing a figure huddled in a sleeping bag, Tempest sent a warming tingle their way, and followed it with a blessing prayer. There must not have been enough space in the warming shelters tonight. Or for some reason, the sidewalk felt safer. Tempest understood that feeling. Sometimes four walls, no matter how warm, could be terrifying things. She still wished she had another blanket to pile on the curled-up form.

She walked up Hawthorne for a bit, ignoring the cars

driving by, past the cheery neon of the 1920s movie theater and restaurant. Then it was past the brick club on the corner, where there weren't even any smokers outside the metal show. Too damn cold. She waited for the light to change and crossed, heading north when she got to the next side street. The one that would take her home.

Her garage apartment wasn't far from the Inner Eye. A pleasant walk just five blocks down some tree-lined streets. She hurried on, aiming her boots toward home. The air changed around her half a block up the street. Becoming quiet. So quiet. Her entire body sighed with relief. She'd really been on edge, and even within the shop wards, smiling at customers all day had been a bit of a strain.

Holiday lights twinkled around her, coaxing out a smile. Portlanders in this neighborhood sure loved their decorations. Tempest liked them, too, which surprised her a little. The Christmas season was always a disappointment to her, growing up. But since finding the coven and beginning to celebrate Solstice—or the Yule season, as some of them called it—the whole winter holiday thing had grown on her.

Light in the dark of the year and all that. It felt like a good thing.

After hearing about the attack on her home, Brenda had done a quick scan of Tempest's energy field and started working with her on mending her *personal* wards. The ones that protected her energy bodies. Turned out there was a small tear in her outer edges, and that was part of the problem. When Tempest had dealt with the apartment wards, she hadn't even thought to check her own. Rookie mistake. Especially since she knew all of those systems were connected. Theoretically, at least. But getting all of her parts to really understand the theories? And put them into practice? Well, she was working on that.

Speaking of... Tempest sent a breath down through the soles of her feet, saying a friendly hello to the sidewalk and all the systems below. Breathing energy up through her feet, she imagined it cycling through her whole body. Practicing with eyes open, and while walking, was something Raquel and Brenda drilled into the whole coven. It was easy enough when Tempest was doing massage, but in ordinary moments, when her thoughts wanted to swirl or her emotions were activated, she still found it hard.

An opossum waddled quickly across the street, white fur lit by the dim yellow of a streetlight. The streets down here were usually quite dark. The streetlamps set far apart, and the light fractured by the massive bare elm branches. She wondered if the holiday lights bothered the nocturnal animals.

Tempest watched the possum disappear behind a low hedge, then went back to her practice. She loosened her gait, letting her arms swing naturally, then breathed into her center, exhaling out to the very edges of her newly shored-up aura.

Center and circumference. She imagined her conscious awareness reaching out three hundred and sixty degrees, the way she'd been taught.

And heard footsteps behind her. Heavy boots, walking quietly. And a whiff of incense resin. Benzoin? And a feeling. A bad, bad, feeling.

Shit.

Tempest increased her pace. Because she'd stopped to watch the possum, Joshua's house—and her apartment—was still two blocks away. And no one else was around.

Besides, she might not make it up her stairs in time. And she really didn't want to lead whoever this was directly home.

Her mind raced through options. Run? Bang on one of the decorated doors and hope someone was there? Dogleg it back to Hawthorne? Face whomever it was?

Tempest's heart pounded and sweat prickled down her spine, despite the near freezing cold. She walked even faster. Throttling down panic, she forced her attention back to the edges of her aura.

It was him. The man from her vision. She couldn't prove it without turning around and looking into his eyes, but her whole body *knew* it. There was that same sense of arrogance. Of cruel, self-centered disregard.

She had to get out of there. Fast.

Tempest walked straight ahead, as quickly as she could, then cheated left down a cross street at the last moment. And ran. A surge of anger smacked her energy field, and she stumbled in her boots, but caught herself. She put on a burst of speed, arms and legs pumping, backpack bouncing against her lower back. Her damn insulated coat was too tight around her upper thighs, but there was no time to unzip it, so she rucked it up around her hips.

Turned left again, pelting back toward Hawthorne. Too far from the shop. What was down here? What would be open?

Cars rushed by. She slammed to a stop, teetering on the sidewalk's edge. There. Across the street, half a block up. A bar.

A sliver opened up in the two lanes on her side and Tempest ran, barely pausing at the center to check for cars driving the other way. Clear.

She ran, not looking back, side aching, until her gloved hands smacked the wooden door and slammed it up against the wall.

Breath heaving, she stumbled inside, moving toward the

light that gleamed from the shelved bottles at the back of the bar.

"Tempest?" A voice she recognized.

"Tempest? Satan's balls, are you okay?" Another voice. Daniel's. Daniel was here.

She turned.

And Ruby. Ruby was here.

"Outside. Being followed."

Ruby's red lips set in an angry line. She spun on her boots and slammed out the door. Two people Tempest didn't know—a huge man and small, round woman —followed.

Daniel held out his arms. She fell into them, sobbing with relief.

18

RUBY

Angry. She was fucking angry.

She yanked open the heavy wood door, barely aware of Sean and Carla closing in behind. Running out onto the sidewalk, the cold smacked her, but she didn't care.

Her head swiveled. Cars. A couple walking arm-in-arm a block away.

Other direction. Nothing. Red light two blocks down. Cars waiting.

Crossing the street, blond hair reflecting streetlights on one side, and darkness on the other. He caught sight of her and smiled.

"Hey! Dickhead!" Ruby shouted. "What the fuck do you think you're doing?'

The tall, razor-thin man sauntered the rest of the way across the four lanes, as if he had no care in the world.

A big hand fell on her shoulder. Sean. Carla tucked up at her side. Nudged her arm. "I brought your coat. Put it on."

Ruby didn't turn. Didn't take her eyes off the man heading toward them. But she felt the coat in her hands and shrugged her way into it.

He was close now. So close.

There was a weird, burning smell around him. It cut through the cold and the lingering traces of car exhaust and oil. Some sort of incense?

He stopped a yard away. Too close for comfort, but outside of punching range. For her, at least. Maybe Sean could reach him. As if he'd heard her, she felt Sean shift from just behind her shoulder to standing at her side. He still allowed her a few inches ahead of his bulk, to show she was in the lead. Good man, Sean.

The thoughts barely flickered across her mind. She focused on Blond Asshole's eyes. In this light, they were washed out, with barely any color around the dark pupils. That damn lock of wheat-blond hair fell across his forehead. He pushed at it, holding her gaze. Still smiling.

"I asked you a question," Ruby said. "What the fuck do you think you're doing?"

He shrugged. Nonchalant. "Just taking a walk. Thought I might stop in for a beer. Get some sweet potato fries."

"By chasing my friend?"

"Oh, she's your friend now, is she? I had no idea you two knew each other."

She held her eyes on his. Steady. Her cold hands clenched into fists. Sean and Carla shifted around her. Straightening. Taller. A shield wall between this man and the door to the bar. A united front.

"So, you admit you were following her?" Carla said. Her normally cheerful voice sounded like a harbinger of death.

Cars whooshed by. Laughter. Music. Gone into the night. Barely there. The world telescoped down to four figures on a city sidewalk as temperatures dropped.

Ruby swallowed. Tasted the ghost of bourbon on her

tongue. She spared a thought for Tempest. She'd looked so small and fierce and scared. Scared by this piece of shit.

This piece of shit that had planted some sort of damn Nazi spell in her booth. Her teeth ground together. Before she could think, she had worked a wad of spit up and hawked it at his shiny-booted feet.

She saw him flinch, just for a second, before the smirk reestablished itself on his face.

"Classy."

"You should leave."

"Not until I talk to your 'friend'." Pale fingers made air quotes around the final word.

"You don't need to talk to anyone, buddy." Sean's voice rumbled, not quite a growl, but a clear warning. "You just need to leave."

"Last I heard, I had a right to assemble, and a right to speak. Isn't that what all of you left wing freaks are saying all the time?"

"You can go freely assemble and talk to yourself somewhere else." A stiff breeze started up, whipping Ruby's hair around her face, and feathering the damn blond lock on Nazi Asshole's head. She hoped his close shaved scalp felt like ice. It looked like it. His thin lips were practically fading into his white skin.

He feigned right. Sean stepped out to block him. Backing up, the man stepped left. Ruby felt Carla move. She herself stood, stable. The frost she felt gathering in the air filled her lungs. Inside herself, the cold grew into a certainty. This asshole was afraid.

Ruby stepped toward him. Just one step. Felt him flinch again.

She leaned closer. There was barely two feet between

them now. She could smell incense and some sour skin smell, as if he needed a good scrub. Probably did.

"You really should go somewhere else."

"Oh yeah? And why's that?"

"Because. We don't like you."

He huffed out an incredulous breath, and rolled his shoulders, as if getting ready for a fight. Well, let him. Craft fair season was over for the year, and Ruby was ready for whatever fight this skinny Nazi wanted to bring.

"Ruby?"

That voice. Soft and small. Coming from behind her.

"Tempest, you really don't want to be out here right now." Ruby raised her voice to carry over her shoulder, still not moving her eyes from the man in front of her.

She felt him relax and straighten. He smiled again, as if he'd just won.

"You haven't won anything, you asshole. So I don't know what you're gloating about. And we still want you to leave."

He was looking past her shoulder now. Not focused on her at all.

"I have a message for your coven," he said.

Ruby made a gesture to her side. Motioning to Sean. He and Carla moved up, shoulder to shoulder with her this time. No tiny gap denoting who was leading this messed-up dance. Just a solid, furious, blockade.

The man in front of her craned his neck and rose up on the balls of his feet.

"Tell them to leave Portland business to Portland businesses."

What? Confusion filled her mind. That was so not what she expected.

"What?" Tempest's voice echoed Ruby's thought. "I have

no idea what you're talking about. I just want you to leave me alone."

"I'll leave you alone as soon as you fucking witches leave the normal citizens of Portland alone. Fucking hippy punks. People are just trying to get along, you know? Stop your damn interference."

"Or what?" Ruby asked. Her voice felt like a blade. Sharp. As if it could cut through steel. Sean was a blazing furnace to one side, and Carla was solid as a stone. And behind that? The flickering light of Tempest. A woman she didn't even know.

"Or you'll all have to deal with me."

Ruby laughed, shattering the tension. "Are you kidding me?"

She shoved his shoulders. He huffed and backed up, surprise flashed across his face. "Who the fuck do you think you are? Some big, scary, Libertarian Satanist Wannabe? I know Satanists who will kick your skinny white ass. I know anarchists who can eat your bones for breakfast. Get the fuck out of here."

He shoved her back. Hard. She rocked backward, stopped by one Sean's big arms. Ruby repositioned her boots on the concrete. Shook out her arms.

"You don't want to do that," Sean growled. "You really, really don't."

And then Tempest was there, at Ruby's side, fists clenched, tiny body shaking. How the fuck had she gotten around Sean?

The witch held her hands up, palms flat, facing out. Her hands barely reached above the level of his shoulders, but it didn't matter. Ruby could feel her rage. Her power.

Tempest flicked her fingers three times. Ruby could have sworn she saw sparks, though that wasn't possible.

"You want to take on witches, huh?" Tempest's voice was tight, harsh, straining against her vocal cords. "You want to take on our magic? You want to face a whole city full of backup? Cause that's what we've got."

Tempest dropped her arms. The weird tension snapped. Broke.

All of a sudden, they were just a group of people, standing on a sidewalk on a cold, winter's night.

"Fuck you." The man spat the words at Tempest, but Ruby could tell there was no heat in them. Only spite.

He turned heel and left.

It should have felt like a victory, but Ruby wasn't counting any chickens. Not yet.

She knew that spite was an effective mask for rage.

And rage was a dangerous thing.

19

TEMPEST

Tempest's whole body shook, and not from the cold. He just...walked away, striding down the sidewalk as if he owned it, back toward Cesar Chavez Boulevard. There was no sound. And everything seemed to be moving in slow motion.

Body pumped full of adrenaline, her thoughts raced through her head like lightning. She couldn't believe it. She hadn't even done anything. Not really. She'd just raised her arms. Flicked her fingers. She didn't even know why she'd done that. It just felt right. But it had actually *done* something. Like...

She didn't even know. Like maybe... *Diana, was that you?*

Before an answer came, a wave of exhaustion crashed through her and she slumped. The sound of cars. Voices. Too loud. She covered her ears with her hands. They felt like blocks of ice attached to the ends of her arms. The air was so cold. Too cold. Where were her gloves?

"Tempest! Are you okay?" Who? Scent of bourbon and sweet breath. Ruby.

Daniel, suddenly in front of her. Gently prying her

hands from her ears. "Tempest. You're safe. You did great. Let's get you inside. You're freezing."

She let herself be turned. The big man, Sean, held the bar door open. His wife? Carla. Right. Carla. She was at the bar, talking urgently to the bartender. The music seemed too loud, but the dim lights were good. Safe. And Daniel was right. It was warm in here. Tempest's head nodded. It was all she could do to keep her eyes open. She really just wanted to sleep.

"What's happening to her?" Ruby's voice again. Worried.

Daniel steered her to a booth and helped her slide her way in. It felt good to have the tall wood bench at her back. To feel Daniel's body heat next to her. He grabbed her hands and placed them inside his own. His hands were cold, but not as cold as hers.

Ruby slid in across the table.

"Carla's getting you some mint tea. We should order you some food, too. Is there anything you can't eat? Something that sounds good?"

Tempest focused on Ruby's face. She looked angry. Worried. Fierce. Her red lipstick was smeared a bit near the bottom edge. She'd taken off her jacket and wore a cranberry-red sweater that made her skin glow, even in the low lights of the bar.

Tempest finally realized the woman must have asked her something, because Ruby was just looking at her. Waiting.

"What did you say?"

"I said Carla's bringing you some tea to warm you up. But I feel like we should get some food into you. You're really not looking so hot. Does anything sound good?"

Tempest's eyes really wanted to close. Damn it. Her body was shutting down. She wanted sleep.

"I just want to sleep."

"Does this happen to her often?" Ruby asked Daniel. Why wasn't she asking her? Tempest closed her eyes. Her mind still worked, but her body didn't want to. Too much effort.

"I'm not really sure. I know she has chronic fatigue. Some sort of chronic illness. But I thought she was getting a little better lately."

He shifted in the booth next to her. "Hey, Tempest?" His voice was gentle. Soft. That was nice. "Didn't you say there was something you were doing lately that had started helping you? A new medication or something? Do you have it on you? Can you take some now?"

She opened her eyes again, blinking. Daniel and Ruby were both looking at her, and Carla had arrived with a little brown pot of steaming tea. Sean towered behind her, holding a brown glazed mug.

"Oh. Yeah. My CBD. Backpack."

"Where's her backpack?" Ruby asked.

Carla hoisted it from a coat hook at the end of the booth and passed it to Daniel, who unzipped the main pocket and held it out for Tempest.

"Front pocket," she said. He unzipped that, too. She rooted around, hands closing on a small glass bottle safely hidden in an inner pocket. She shook it, drew out the dropper filled with dark, viscous liquid, and squirted it onto her tongue.

Closing her eyes again, she felt someone's hands—Ruby's?—gently take the bottle from her. She tasted the sweet, oily cannabis, and swallowed, praying as she did so that the plant would do its work.

Meanwhile… "Tea? And a hamburger with salad, no bun, no tomatoes. Just vinegar and oil. Please?"

"On it," Sean said, and turned to head back to the bar.

Ruby poured some tea into the mug and slid it across to Tempest. Their fingers brushed during the transfer. Tempest looked up, startled. Ruby smiled.

"That should help."

It smelled like mint and licorice. The thick ceramic was warm, almost hot, but not quite. She wrapped her fingers around it. Grateful.

"Thank you."

"Is the CBD helping?" Daniel asked.

Tempest paused. Considered. "It doesn't really work that way. I think it's cumulative but...huh." The heightened sense of danger and anxiety that had pumped through her since she first heard the footsteps behind her and began to run had softened around the edges. It was as if her animal self was finally calming down. Not still flooding her with adrenaline and exhausting her even more.

"Yeah," she said. "It is helping. It's taken the edge off. I'm not in a panic anymore."

He rubbed his hand across her back. "That's good. Now drink your tea."

20

RUBY

Ruby sipped at her now-watered-into-oblivion bourbon. The ice had melted while they dealt with asshole outside. She was trying not to stare at the woman across from her, who sawed into her hamburger patty, shoveling fork into mouth as if she had just run a marathon or was half starving. Sean and Carla chatted quietly at the end of the booth, and Daniel was busy typing something on his phone.

There were still a few other people in the place. She could hear their quiet laughs and conversation, and jazz still played over the speakers, as if it was just a normal Sunday evening. As if something dangerous and momentous hadn't just happened outside half an hour before.

What the fuck, anyway? How had life gotten so damn weird?

She'd been going along, having some fun, dating a few women, building her business, and trying to keep from having to get a second job. And then, in just a few days, she had been threatened by a Nazi Satanist and was falling for a witch who had some sort of weird illness.

And some sort of strange power. Ruby couldn't deny it. First of all, there was the way Tempest had captured her imagination since the second she first saw her at Cider Revolution. And then there was tonight. Watching this small woman take on Nazi Boy was just...damn. She'd simply stepped out in front of their cadre and stared the man down. Then she'd raised her arms, flicked her fingers, and something happened. Ruby had no idea what, but she saw the naked fear that flashed across his pale eyes.

Maybe it was all psychological, and that was probably the case, but whatever it was had worked. And then Tempest had slumped as if she was a balloon and all the air had rushed out. Both Ruby and Daniel had freaked a bit at that. Luckily, they'd done enough actions to know to stay calm, and Carla and Sean were still around. They were both good caretakers. Ruby was glad to know them.

"Better?" Ruby asked Tempest as soon as she had paused long enough to wipe her mouth and spear some lettuce. The hamburger patty was gone.

"Better." Tempest gave her a shy smile.

"So, what happened out there?"

Tempest chewed and shook her head.

"I'm not exactly sure. One minute I was in here, crying on Daniel's shoulder." She bumped him with her arm and he looked up, distracted, then bent back to his phone. "And the next minute, I was running outside, shoving past you guys and getting in his face."

Tempest paused to drink some tea. It was the second refill. Carla had insisted that she needed more hot liquid inside. Ruby would have already been to the toilets twice, but Tempest seemed to be metabolizing it all okay. She either had a huge bladder, or Carla was right, and she was dehydrated or something.

"I didn't even think about it. It was as if something else took me over, used me, and then cast me aside. Either that, or it was just the adrenaline. That happens to me sometimes."

Ruby raised an eyebrow. "I don't get it. What do you mean?"

"I get adrenaline spikes and crashes. Part of my chronic illness is that my body thinks it's constantly under attack, so it wears down all my systems, including my thyroid and adrenals, compromising my immune system. It also means I don't have steady levels of anything, really. A rush of adrenaline—or even eating the wrong food—can lead to a sudden collapse. I just don't have the reserves like other people do. So after a spike, my body just shuts down."

"That must suck."

"It really does. I'm better than I was, though."

"Because of the CBD?" Which was also weird, but no weirder than anything else going on.

"Yeah. Some things that just weren't healing before are starting to. It's calming my whole system down, plus helps with general stress."

"Hey! One of my comrades figured it out!" Daniel slapped his phone on the table.

"Figured what out?" Sean rumbled.

"That thing the asshole was saying? About the coven, and the business association downtown?"

Tempest dropped her fork on her plate and turned toward Daniel. Ruby could practically feel the change around her. It was as if her whole attention had focused again.

"What about it?" Ruby asked. "I had no idea what he was on about."

"The guy is Brad Chadwick. Son of Martin Chadwick."

He looked as if they should know who the hell he was talking about.

Sean just groaned and stood. "For this, I'm gonna need another drink. You okay to drive, Carla?"

Carla rolled her eyes and blew him a kiss. "Of course, darling."

"Anyone else need another round?"

Ruby looked down at her watered-down drink and nodded. "Another Maker's?"

Daniel shook his head. "I'm good, man."

Sean headed off and Ruby turned her attention back to Daniel, who fidgeted across from her. Tempest was still staring at him, clutching her tea mug now, waiting.

"I don't get it. Who is that?" Ruby really had no clue, but if both Sean and Daniel knew, clearly she should, too.

"The man who wants to be head of the Downtown Business Association but keeps getting voted down. Vocal member, though." He turned back to Tempest. "That group must hate your coven's guts!"

Tempest sat back with a jerk. "Oh, man. Really? But his dad must hate him, right? I mean, look at him?"

Daniel's face was lit with glee. "Oh, no. That's just it. Turns out that daddy's a racist piece of shit. He proudly uses little Brad's upside-down pentagram as a sign that he's religiously tolerant, even though everyone knows he won't hire Muslims and seems to have a special beef with Somalis."

Ruby was still confused, but Sean was back with her bourbon. She raised it in a toast. "Thanks."

He clinked back.

"I still don't get it. Why would the business association have anything to do with your coven?"

Tempest sighed. "Arrow and Crescent helped head up that big action last February, remember? When the houseless community downtown was slated to be torn down and disbanded?"

"Oh, yeah. Right. I was out of town for that but heard about it."

"Well, the Downtown Business Association were some of the main proponents of trashing the camp. And some of them had ties to the big developer that was torching buildings for insurance a year ago. My coven mate Cassiel worked on bringing that to a stop."

Ruby quirked an eyebrow. "I heard some rumor about a ghost? Some dead journalist? You're not telling me all that was real?"

Daniel and Tempest both just stared at her, and Carla cleared her throat.

"Real or not, Cassie definitely took that bastard down. How Mayor Patterson didn't lose his job over that one, I'm still not sure."

"Damn," Tempest said. "I've really got to get the coven on this now. I was hoping my vision was just…"

Sean reached a hand toward Tempest, though it didn't quite reach down the booth. He left it resting there. "We all have visions, lass. Just some of us don't pay them any mind. You'd best pay attention to this one, sounds like."

Well, shit. Even Sean was on board.

She had really hoped—much as she was attracted to the pale woman in her goldenrod- and black-striped scarf—that this was going to turn out to be nothing but nonsense after all. She looked down at the golden brown liquid in the short, clear glass.

She had a business to save. And a real life LARP? Well, she hadn't LARPed in years.

When she raised the glass to her lips for a drink, she

noticed Daniel staring at her. Giving her a look, as if he could tell she was squirming again.

He didn't say anything, just raised an eyebrow, then turned away to talk to Sean.

She ignored Daniel and took a sip of bourbon. It tasted smooth, like caramel, but it burned like fire going down.

Tempest was looking at her now, with those big, dark eyes. And in the middle of the table, the Black Sun glowed dully in the lights of the bar. She wrapped it back up in red tissue paper and shoved it into the gift bag.

No one but Tempest even noticed.

Damn, again. Who did she think she was fooling? She already was *in* a fucking LARP. Sitting in a tavern with witches and a magic amulet practically wrapped up with a bow.

Preparing to do battle.

21

TEMPEST

Tempest padded, dressed in slippers, pajamas, and her oversized yellow hoodie, toward the small living room area of her apartment. Yellow had been her favorite color ever since she first read those books about a boy wizard and a magical school. That had been a particularly bad time, when she was on the verge of running again. Those books got her through. They helped her run without running, by taking her away from her life. Tempest had wanted a way to be brave even though she needed her cloak of invisibility in order to remain safe.

Tempest wanted someone or something trustworthy enough to be loyal to.

She didn't talk about those books much anymore. The author had spoken up publicly too many times in ways that hurt Tempest's friends—especially people she truly loved and counted on, like Selene. But wrapping herself in yellow was still a comfort. It cheered her up. Gave her courage. Besides, no one could take a story away from a reader. Not even the one who wrote it.

At least, that's what Selene said when Tempest had asked them about it.

Graymalkin followed her, butting his head against her calf. Curtains closed against the cold winter night, the space was lit with warm light from one of her bedside lamps and a floor lamp donated by her coven mate Lucy, who sometimes got cast-offs from fancy homes who had hired her firm to repaint in the midst of some decorating frenzy.

Tempest was bone tired, but her brain wouldn't shut up. Ruby had insisted on driving her home, even though it had taken almost as long to walk to where Ruby's car was parked as it would have taken Tempest to walk home. All the same, she appreciated it. Being followed like that still rattled her nerves.

But another thing that rattled her nerves? Ruby. When they'd pulled up in front of Joshua's house, and Tempest's small abode, the woman had actually asked her out.

Like, on a date.

Tempest had flushed, thankful the car was dark and Portland streetlights were notoriously weak and spaced far apart. She'd stammered out some string of words that must have approximated a "yeah, sure," because next thing she knew, she'd agreed to dinner.

Tempest flopped onto the big brown chair and curled up. As soon as she settled, Graymalkin jumped into her lap, kneaded her thigh for two minutes, then settled into her lap and closed his eyes.

She scratched his head. "Do you think I should go on a date, boy?"

He slitted his orange eyes at her for a second, then closed them again and began to purr.

The date was really the least of her worries. Tempest needed to alert the rest of the coven, but it was—she pulled her phone from her hoodie pocket—eleven o'clock on a Sunday night. Raquel woke up at o-dark-thirty because of the café, and Brenda was probably just heading to bed herself. Besides, everyone had partners and were probably snuggled up, watching movies, or sleeping, or...yeah. Having sex.

That thing that dates were supposed to lead to. That thing Tempest avoided, despite being in her early twenties and everyone assuming.

When you'd had to ward off assholes from age ten on, willingly letting someone get close enough to take your clothes off? Yeah. Right.

And she hadn't always been successful in warding them off. Hadn't always gotten away in time. She'd never been actually "raped" but...what had happened to her was bad enough.

She'd never gotten the chance to experiment like other teenagers. Oh, she'd fooled around a tiny bit. Some kissing, mostly. But she'd never willingly taken her clothes off with anyone. She'd always been too scared. Plus, she moved around a lot, and disappeared into the walls as much as possible. It was the only way to keep safe.

But now? With Ruby? Did she want to?

That was the thing. She thought she might want to. But she also got the feeling that Ruby had a ton of experience. What if she didn't want some inexperienced dork?

Tempest's eyes roamed toward the small wood table set under the window, with its current backdrop of navy curtains. Her magical tools were arrayed neatly on top. A cup. A blade. An incense burner. A willow wand. A double-bladed knife that she'd paid Brenda one penny for because, even though it was a gift, "You always have to pay for a knife," her mentor said.

Pride of place, in the center of the altar, was her statue of Diana the Hunter, crescent bow upraised to shoot the moon.

"What do you think, Diana? People say you're a virgin, too. Brenda and Raquel say that just means a person is complete unto themself. Sovereign. Whole."

And Selene, Moss, Lucy, and Alejandro all just said that the idea of virginity was a crock of garbage and no one should even use that word anymore.

"Have sex, or don't have sex," Moss had said. "But it has nothing to do with your identity or worth. A person who has a lot of sex has just as much worth and sovereignty as someone who hasn't had any."

"Virginity? Patriarchal bullshit," was Selene's reply.

Tempest smiled. Her coven mates were awesome.

Which brought her wandering thoughts back to the other thing keeping her awake despite having massage clients the next day. Brad Chadwick and that threat he'd leveled at Arrow and Crescent Coven.

And her response. That strange, outpouring of power she'd felt, and then the complete deflation, feeling as if all of her reserves were drained.

"You really should be in bed, asleep," she told herself. Her fingernails ticked at her phone case. They looked short, but clearly needed a good trim before she got her hands near anyone's bare skin.

Who could she talk to, this late at night?

Alejandro. He was always up late, and with his partner, Shekinah, and boyfriend, Thomas, there was an equal chance he was either busy or free. Tempest found polyamory funny that way. People always talked about scheduling issues, but in Tempest's observation, Alejandro was more likely to have a free night than her coven mates with one steady partner, who seemed always spoken for.

She woke up her phone and dialed.

Three rings in, his voice spoke in her ear.

"You're not busy, are you?"

Graymalkin stretched and resettled in her lap, and Tempest settled in for what might be a long conversation.

She had a lot to explain. And it was clear, the coven really needed to get on board.

As for Ruby and the question of sex?

Well, she guessed she had to get through a proper date first.

She'd never been on one before.

22

RUBY

It was snowing.

Not a heavy, dumping snow like the Pacific Northwest got on the mountain passes, but a light, gentle falling of white dust from the sky. It was gloriously beautiful, and the only reason Ruby was happy to be awake and en route to brunch. She always slept in the day after a con or craft fair, as a reward for working her ass off for several days in a row. Add in the weird drama of the weekend that had started on...Friday? Wow. That seemed like a week ago already. At any rate, between the Patriots at the cidery, Libertarian Satanist Boy showing up at Geeks and Bells, and then chasing Tempest down last night? Ruby was a jittery, queasy combination of exhausted and wired.

Luckily, the vegan brunch spot she was meeting Lawrence at had good coffee with free refills and house-made walnut milk. She wasn't picky about her dairy-like substances, but quality was quality. Right?

The air smelled fresh. Crisp. The tiny flakes of snow dotted Ruby's cheeks. She smiled. There was just nothing better than the first snowfall, before the sun had come out and melted it, and then it refroze overnight into a deadly layer of ice. She was thankful for the all wheel drive on her hatchback, that was for sure. She had found a parking spot a few blocks from the restaurant, just down from the Station, where they'd been the night before.

It was funny: Ruby almost never came to this neighborhood, preferring her stomping grounds in the northeast, but all of a sudden, here she was again.

"Some witchy vortex," she muttered. But her heart beat a little faster at the thought that she just might bump into Tempest on the street. Maybe she was working at the shop today. Ruby would have to ask Lawrence.

She shoved her gloved hands into her coat pockets and felt something that shouldn't be there.

Damn it. It was the folded-up gift bag with the amulet. In all the confusion and weirdness of last night, Daniel hadn't taken it.

Whipping out her phone, she tapped out a text.

En route. Need to talk to Daniel, too. OK to invite?

Three tiny dots bubbled up on the screen.

Sure. If he's around.

Ruby grinned. Daniel was as a notorious slut as she was. Or she had been, until recently. He very well might be otherwise occupied on a freaking cold Monday morning. Or he might be at work, though she didn't think so. She seemed to recall that he had Mondays off for some reason.

Great. Almost there.

She fired off a text to Daniel. If he couldn't meet her this morning, maybe they could get together that night. Tempest had said she had some coven thing to go to but had promised to set a time for a date soon.

Ruby really hoped that was true.

23

———

TEMPEST

The snow was just wonderful, just right for a post-brunch, Monday walk.

Tempest had wrapped her huge scarf three times around her neck. Between that and her matching wool watch cap pulled down as far as it would go, most of her face was covered. She had on long underwear, jeans, boots, a long-sleeved T-shirt, and a fleece zip-up, all so she could wear her vintage leather coat. The warmer insulated coat was a lot more practical, but Tempest felt more like herself in the short, vintage bomber jacket.

And today? She desperately needed to feel like herself.

With almost no cars on Hawthorne, she and her coven mate Selene may as well have been walking in a small village. Stiff red ribbons decorated the lamp posts, and shop windows were painted with holly or edged with fake frost. The bare-limbed trees were dusted in white, as were the shop awnings and the few cars parked along the sidewalk. They passed a proprietor setting out a no-slip mat in front of the door to a botanicals shop. Twinkle lights lined the shop window, glowing brightly.

"Good morning!" the shopkeeper said.

They responded in kind and kept going.

"I don't get what the problem is," Selene continued, picking up the thread of conversation they'd started over eggs and toast at Dish and Spoon. "With Ruby, I mean, not with the asshole stalker. The coven definitely needs to deal with that."

Selene looked gorgeous as always. They'd spent the night at Joshua's place, so it had been easy to score the last-minute breakfast date, since that meant Selene was literally down the driveway from Tempest's garage abode, and close to Dish and Spoon. They were walking now because, though brunch had been delicious and they'd lingered over second cups of coffee, Selene had more to say.

Selene's lips were painted a deep plum this morning, in contrast with their snowy white skin. Eyes lined in kohl, eyebrows plucked into arches, black scarf wound around their neck beneath a long, black wool coat. While others in the coven wore a wide variety of colors, Selene was a Goth femme to the core.

The non-binary witch's energy always made Tempest feel at ease. Where other coven members worried about Tempest—or wanted to help her improve some of her life conditions—sometimes they could act like annoying parental units.

Selene wasn't as young as Tempest and Moss but was in the middle ground of ages along with Tobias. The others edged toward their forties or were firmly in the middle of them.

Being the youngest member of the coven, Tempest didn't want to always feel like the baby, or the mascot, or the one who needed to be taken care of. Dealing with her illness and her past was enough. She didn't need to always stave off people's worry, too, much as she knew they loved her.

Sometimes she wanted to be around someone who just let her be. Selene was that person.

"So, what are you afraid of with this situation? If she's into you, and you're into her, what's the harm in just going on a date? Check things out."

The continuous light dusting had grown thick enough on the sidewalk for their boots to leave impressions.

"That all makes sense. You know. In my head," Tempest replied. "But gah! People like her just freak me out! She's so...bright. Confident. Sure of herself."

"And? You're pretty terrific yourself, Tempest. You care about people. You're working hard on your massage business..."

"I'm a sickly, shy dork of a witch. And I'm a virgin!" She hissed out that last word, sending a puff of steam into the frigid air.

Selene stopped in their tracks and turned toward Tempest, causing a bundled-up man to veer suddenly around them.

"I thought we talked about that. About what patriarchal bullshit that is. It's your body, you do what you want with it, and there's nothing wrong with that."

"So you say. But who the hell hasn't had sex by my age?" Tempest's face burned so hot she was sure she could melt snow. The coffee and eggs roiled uneasily in her stomach. Damn it. She hadn't had a panic attack in a year. She really didn't want one now. She willed herself to breathe.

Selene just shrugged as if they didn't notice that Tempest was freaking out. They resumed walking. "I'm sure there are plenty of people. Look, I get that the thought of physical intimacy when you haven't really gone there before could seem intimidating. I don't want to make light of that. But, if not with this person, who sounds pretty great, then who?"

"I don't know." Now Tempest felt like she was whining, but at least the sense of panic had died down. "I guess you're right. So, you think I should go on this date?"

Selene shot her another glance. "It's up to you, but yeah. I think you should."

As they walked, the snow had stopped, and the clouds cleared just enough for the sun to break through. The street was truly gorgeous now. And so was...

"Oh my Goddess!" Tempest stopped, then stepped out of the way of a parent pushing a tricked-out jogging stroller. Her mouth was dust dry. Walking down the street, just a few blocks away, was a woman with hair as dark as Selene's poking out from beneath a cherry-red wool hat. It was Ruby. Her head was bent toward her phone. Texting. Good. That meant she hadn't seen them yet.

What was she doing in the neighborhood on a Monday morning? She lived in northeast, right?

"What? What happened?" Selene looked around, confusion wrinkling their forehead.

"It's her."

"Really? Which one? Red hat?"

Tempest just nodded, riveted in place.

"Oooh. She *is* cute. Dang, girl!" Selene bumped Tempest with their hip, which, given Selene's height, hit her waist.

Damn it, Diana! Tempest knew she needed to deal with this situation. She knew she needed to suck it up and invoke some courage. But she really did not think she was going to have to deal right now.

Or maybe she didn't.

Ruby paused in front of a restaurant, looked in the window, then swung open the door.

Crisis averted.

"This feels like serendipity, doesn't it?" Selene asked. "Shall we go say hi?"

"No way," Tempest replied.

Selene looked at her, one sharp black eyebrow raised. "Does this mean you aren't going to agree to a date?"

Tempest threw up her hands. "All right! All right! I'll text her. Set something up! I promise!"

Selene laughed, the sound bright, crackling through the cold winter air.

Tempest felt slightly ill. And excited. Butterflies? Is that what people were always talking about?

Yeah. Here, on a freezing cold Portland sidewalk, with her coven mate laughing at her, she felt butterflies as if it were spring.

Her phone buzzed in her pocket. She fumbled it out with gloved fingers.

"It's Moss."

The smile slid off of Selene's face.

"What's he say?"

Tempest looked at the words on her phone, butterflies replaced by the ice of fear.

"He did some research on my stalker. It might be worse than we thought."

"And?

"He wants to meet up, but I can't. I have two clients today!"

She ripped off her gloves with her teeth and thumbed her message back, staring at the small screen until his reply came back.

"He'll give us a full report tonight. Coven meeting.

Another damn emergency coven meeting right before a major holiday." She looked at Selene, whose plum-coated mouth tipped down into a frown. "When will this stuff let up? We've barely had a break."

"We're freaks, Tempest. Freaks who care. And that means we'll always have work to do." They sighed. "But yeah, it sure would be nice to just celebrate together once in a while, wouldn't it? After all the victories we've had? We deserve some time to rest."

But that wasn't going to happen. And, tension roiling in her belly, Tempest really feared what Moss was going to say. Just great. Now how in Diana's name was she supposed to get through her day?

She heard the echo of Brenda's voice in her ear.

One breath at a time.

24

RUBY

The mismatched wooden booths and tables sat in what could have been a cavernous industrial space, but somehow managed to feel homey. The steel beams were painted a pale blue, and giant glass chandeliers hung from the high ceilings. The clatter of dishes and sounds of cooking came through the open kitchen hatch, blending with the sleepy late-morning conversations all around them.

Ruby and Lawrence sat across from each other at a table near one of the big plate glass windows that looked out onto the street and the softly falling snow. They tucked into their winter vegetable hash. Ruby's had smoked tempeh for protein, but Lawrence's was topped with two runny eggs that he was currently cutting up, making a general yolky mess of his entire plate.

"That looks disgusting, dude," she said, setting her fork down to take a sip of her beloved coffee.

He grinned up at her. "Yeah, but it tastes so good."

Daniel came skidding into the restaurant, unwinding his ratty blue scarf and unzipping his hooded coat. He waved and went to order at the counter, coming back with a cup of coffee of his own.

"What's up with me always being late for food this week?"

"I know," Lawrence chided. "That's unlike you, man."

"Maybe you all just need to get better about inviting me before you start eating." He wrapped his fingers around the heavy white mug and sighed. "Damn, its cold. My skinny Asian ass can't take this."

Lawrence shrugged. "I like it." He proceeded to shove more of the eggy mess into his face.

Daniel looked to Ruby for backup. She shrugged, too.

"My wide Asian ass likes the cold just fine. Better than sweating. Besides, I make my living selling scarves and shawls, so it works out for me."

Or she was trying to make a living selling scarves and shawls. Damn it. So much for taking the day off from work. She really needed to start going through her records from the weekend. See how much money actually came in.

A cute Black waiter plopped down a plate of biscuits and vegetarian gravy in front of Daniel. The thing was smothered in grilled mushrooms and onions and smelled delicious.

"Thanks, man!" Daniel said.

"Have a blessed day, friend," the waiter replied, before walking away to wipe down a table.

There it was again. The world was just conspiring to get Ruby into the woo. Including the damn amulet, now in her coat pocket. She just couldn't stand to have it that close to her skin. Besides, she'd now been bitten by the metal twice and was done with it.

She gave Daniel a chance to catch up, food wise, and stolidly ate her own hash. The smoked tempeh, yam, greens, and beets, which had tasted so good just moments before, might as well have had no taste for all she was noticing it. If her body didn't still need fuel after the weekend, she would have pushed her plate away.

After Daniel had a couple of bites of biscuit in him, and had downed a quarter of his coffee, he wiped his mouth.

"So. What's up now?"

Ruby sighed and pulled the folded-up gift bag from her coat. She set it on the table, between the salt and pepper shakers. She felt like shit from even touching the bag at this point, though it was probably just her imagination.

Daniel whistled. "Shit! I forgot to take that last night!"

"Yeah. When all the shit went down with that asshole chasing Tempest, I forgot about it, too. Speaking of, there's something else you should know. I think Nazi Brad was at Cider Liberation the other night. Pretty sure he tripped me."

Daniel carefully pulled the now-rumpled red tissue paper from the bag and unfolded it.

"Well, shit. That makes this whole thing even more complicated."

Lawrence held out his left hand around five inches from the Black Sun, face screwed up in concentration. He lowered his hand another couple inches, then pulled it away and shook it off.

"Anyone got hand sanitizer?"

Both Ruby and Daniel shook their heads.

"Be right back." Lawrence shoved his chair back and strode off toward the washrooms.

"Yeah, that is a nasty piece of work," Daniel said. "I'll cover it in salt inside a closed box, but we'll have to figure out something more permanent later."

"I still don't get it. What's going on with these things?"

Daniel picked up his coffee mug and took a long swallow. "It's hard to explain. Especially to Ms. Anti-Magic."

"I'm not anti-magic!" Ruby felt offended, though she wasn't sure why. "After our talk, I'm trying. I really am."

"Yeah? Well, so am I." Daniel's voice was harsh. His words were clipped.

Whoa. That was a smack in the face. She slid the red paper toward her to get a closer look but moved too quickly. The amulet started to slip. She caught it with one finger and shoved it back onto the center of the paper.

"I just meant..." Ruby started. She rubbed her finger on her jeans.

He waved her words away. "It's not you. It's this asshole. I'm just pissed off. Sorry. Don't mean to take it out on you."

Lawrence came back and sat down, then looked from Daniel to Ruby. "Tense much? What the hell happened in the three minutes I was gone?"

"Nothing," Daniel mumbled into his mug. "I'm just a little on edge. And Ruby just touched the damn Black Sun again."

Lawrence sighed, then looked at her. "Ruby, you touched that thing? You should wash your hands."

"Seriously?" Her mind still didn't want to believe it, despite the fact that she'd slathered herself with hand sanitizer after touching it the first time. She'd told herself that was just because it had nicked her. But she'd washed her hands when she got here today, too, hadn't she, after touching the bag? She'd just told herself it was because she was going to eat.

But really? And after touching it for one second just now, her pointer finger felt like it had been coated in some strange oil. And much as she wanted to tell herself that pewter was just an oily feeling metal, she had a feeling that was just so much bullshit.

She wiped her hand on a fresh paper napkin from the dispenser on the table.

"I'll wash it later. But right now, I want to know more about this damn thing and what this guy is up to."

Ruby went to grab her coffee mug and stopped herself. She didn't want to touch anything with that hand, she realized. With a growl, she grabbed the mug with her other hand.

Daniel and Lawrence both just watched her, faces carefully blank.

Ruby set down the mug. "Okay. Okay. I'll go wash my damn hands."

She shoved her chair back with a scrape and threaded her way through the mismatched wooden tables to the toilets. Locking the door behind her, she stared at her reflection in the mirror above the small white sink. The rounded planes of her face looked haunted, surrounded by the reflected backdrop of red- and black-flowered wallpaper behind her.

"What the hell is going on, Rubes? Why are you still fighting this?"

Her reflection had no answer, so she turned on the taps, hit the soap gel dispenser, and scrubbed at her hands with the stinky white soap.

She was in way over her head and hated it. But so far, fighting it was only throwing her back into the same loop, over and over. She kept having this conversation with herself. About not liking the woo. About the world conspiring to surround her with it.

"So learn to deal," she said to her reflection, as her hands scrubbed and scrubbed under the warm flow of water. "Buck up. Either actually treat it like a LARP, with all that entails, or treat it like it's real, because this magic shit isn't going away. And people need your help."

If this was a LARP, that amulet meant she'd taken a hit from this dude, and no way could she allow him to call the shots. The only plan of attack was being formulated by people who could counter magic with magic. She needed to level up. Roll the dice. Increase her spell slots.

Figure out who the damn dungeon master was and follow through.

She turned off the taps, shook off her hands, grabbed two paper towels to dry off with, and headed back into the restaurant.

When she reached the table, she threw the wadded-up paper towels beside her half-eaten breakfast, sat down, picked up her coffee cup, and leaned across the table.

Lawrence and Daniel both looked startled and slightly wary, the way people looked when they'd been caught talking about you when you weren't in the room.

Well, she couldn't blame them.

"Okay. I'm in. Tell me all about this magic or whatever it is. Tell me what you know about this fucked-up Nazi symbol. And tell me what the hell we can do about it. Then, let's roll some fucking dice."

25

TEMPEST

Tempest had gotten through her two Monday massage clients, and they'd both tipped her pretty well, too, so that was something. Backpack in her lap, Tempest looked out the streaky bus window at the tire shops and bars; Charlie's gaming store, Owlbear; and the old seventies-style post office.

The bus rumbled down the road, taking her from the cheap treatment space she rented twice a week back up to her neighborhood and home. If the timing had been right, she would've stopped into Raquel's café to commiserate over a cup of tea, but the café closed at four so Raquel could spend some time with her son, Zion, after school.

It had stopped snowing, and everyone on the bus was all bundled up against the cold. Hats, big coats, scarves, gloves. Up front, a little kid in a bright pink coat read a picture book to their mom. The heat was on, which meant Tempest was sweating, but it didn't feel worth it to take off any of her layers. She unwound her scarf, though, and that helped a little. The scent of damp wool and someone's fast food takeout filled the space.

It was almost four thirty, and outside the bus, the last glimmers of sunset flashed like a knife's edge in the west. The sky was already the deep blue signaling that night was on its way. Coven meeting was at seven thirty. That meant Tempest had time to shower and eat something, maybe chill out with Graymalkin for a bit, before hopping back on a bus to Raquel's house. As if she was going to chill out at all.

She had made it through the day one breath at a time, but the edges of her skin still felt tight, as if she had some sort of psychic sunburn.

The bus turned, rolling past the old arcade and the fancy taco shop. Her stop was coming up. But she didn't pull the cord. It got closer and closer, and her hand didn't reach up. Didn't tug at the plastic-wrapped cable. Didn't signal for the bus to stop.

Finally, last minute, she heard a ding. Someone else had pulled the cord.

But Tempest stayed put. She needed to go see Brenda, she realized. She had to check in with someone before the meeting. Get some shoring up. Or some advice. Or...something.

Three stops later, she practically leapt up from her seat. Backpack in hand, she angled her body sideways to squeeze past a man standing near the door.

"Excuse me," she said. He looked up from his phone, startled, and moved out of her way.

She looked back up toward the front of the bus, where the driver peered at her through the large, rearview mirror. "Thanks!" she shouted, then pushed at the double doors. They resisted, then hissed open, and Tempest's boots were on sidewalk once again.

The cold hit her with a shock after the overheated bus and she took in a heaving breath. Good. The cold was good.

She mashed the crossing button and received a mechanical "Wait!" in return. The snow on the roads was gone, but here on the sidewalk, white patterns of boots and shoes lay like strange lace. The trees were dusted in the crooks of their bare branches.

It was all beautiful, but Tempest had no patience for it. The tight-skinned feeling she'd barely kept at bay all day was in full force, and no matter how deeply she tried to breathe, nothing was working. The pressure just increased. When the light finally changed, it was all she could do to not run, long scarf flapping, to the Inner Eye. She could see its windows, brightly lit in the indigo darkness of the early winter's evening.

It looked beautiful. A warm haven. Another place called home.

But something seemed off. She slowed her gait and approached, sending out her senses, three hundred and sixty degrees, just the way she'd been taught. *Where?*

And then she saw him. Tall. Short blond hair catching colored flashes from the holiday lights in shop windows. A chill ran up her spine.

Brad Chadwick. Nazi Boy. Walking through her neighborhood again. Striding along as if he owned the world.

Her heart raced, and she froze, not sure whether she should pursue him, or run into the shop for help.

Holy Diana. What do I do?

The cold twilight didn't answer, but something tugged at her consciousness, telling her to pay attention.

With one last look at the arrogant back of the receding figure, she tuned in to her body. What was it trying to tell her? Almost of their own accord, her gloved hands began to trace the wood outside the shop door, then the windowsill.

Her backpack hung awkwardly as she bent and crouched, but she paid it little mind.

What was she looking for?

There. Tucked into a chink between two bricks in the low wall beneath the big windows, something gleamed.

Tempest paused, breath huffing white into the frigid air, body vibrating.

"Shh," she told herself. She needed to feel. She needed to sense. She needed to see.

Reaching out with one gloved hand, she prodded the gleaming edge. Metal.

A sense of dread filled her.

Oh, no. Not here.

Bells jangled and the glass door opened, letting out a puff of warm, incense-scented air.

"Tempest?" Brenda asked. Tempest heard the bells chime again. The door shutting. "Are you all right?"

Tempest shook her head, then, with one gloved finger, she worked at the metal edge until enough of it was free to grab hold. Luckily, her fingers were small. She carefully drew out a metal disc and held it up into the light, barely noticing as a slip of white paper fluttered to the sidewalk.

A Black Sun shone dully back at her.

"Nononononono…" Her head shaking, that one-word litany was all her mind could muster. She began to sway. "Nononononono…"

"Tempest!" Brenda's hand gripped her shoulder, steadying her. "What is it? Let's get you inside."

"No!" She turned to her mentor, taking in her beautiful, wise face. The glimmer of silver and moonstone. Dark hair piled on her head. Blue wool tunic. No coat. Not dressed for the cold. "We can't take this inside!"

Startled, Brenda took one step back, then her face changed. Her blue eyes grew steely. "What is it? Show me."

Tempest held out the amulet with one gloved hand.

Brenda bit back a curse, then whirled toward the door. "I'll be right back. Don't move."

As if Tempest ever would or could. As if her feet weren't rooted into place, cemented by trembling fear and anger.

Scanning to see if there was anything else, she saw the white paper, small as a fortune cookie slip. It was half stuck in a puddle of snow melt.

She crouched again to pick it up.

Happy Fucking Holidays, it read.

Tempest flushed, the anger inside her flaring. The asshole had brought this fight into her home.

He was aiming creepy spells at her coven? And at people she knew? Well.

One breath at a damn time, she was going to take him down.

RUBY

Cider Liberation was quiet. Two people played darts behind the pony wall in the little annex near the door to the cidery itself.

A couple of people sat at the wooden bar in the back of the small pub room, past the little high two top tables and stools, heavy coats slung over the backs of their bar chairs. The snow was back, and fell steadily outside, but inside the pub, beneath the golden glow of the lights, everything felt snug and warm. Cozy, even.

And Ruby sat at the one long table against the pub wall with a group of radical Satanists. She wished they were there to play Dungeons & Dragons, or even a round of poker, but here you had it. An impromptu meeting about magic.

It was funny; she'd finally decided to go all in, and here she was, sitting in a group of people who didn't believe magic existed.

Except for Daniel and a tall, gorgeous trans woman named Lilith, most of the ASP Satanists really didn't believe in magic at all. The only things they believed in were antifascism, Black Lives Matter, fuck capitalism, keeping religion out of schools, abortion rights discussions, and government. Not that they really believed in government either. But if they had to have it, keep religion out of it.

Ruby agreed with ASP on all points.

She sipped her cider and watched the conversation. Poor Daniel and Lilith were having a rough time of explaining the magical stuff to the others. Lilith's pale skin reminded her of the snow outside. Her hair was an unnatural fiery red, her makeup was minimal, and she, like everyone else at the table except Ruby in her red sweater, was dressed head to toe in black.

Lilith was pretty hot, actually. If a certain tiny witch with platinum-blond hair hadn't captured Ruby's attention, Ruby would probably make a play for Lilith. She loved tall women. It was nice feeling small some of the time.

An old Pogues album piped through the place, Shane McGowan rasping out something about Cúchulainn. Ruby had asked the owner about the song once and gotten a wayyy too long explanation about Irish heroes and myth cycles.

Ruby dragged her attention back to the conversation, and took a sip of crisp, slightly sweet and tangy Three Arrows cider, their latest distillation.

"He's working magic. I'm telling you. He planted that fucking amulet in Ruby's booth after she told him to fuck off at Geeks and Bells."

"Well, technically, we're not one hundred percent sure it was him..." Ruby said. Though who else could it have been? Especially after his little stalking stunt.

Daniel waved a hand, irritated at the interruption. "Plus, I just got a text that Tempest and Brenda found another one outside the Inner Eye."

Ruby went cold inside. "What? You didn't tell me that!"

Daniel turned to her. "I literally got the text as I was walking through the door. I figured I'd just tell the group."

"He's trying to make good on his threats," Ruby replied. "He said he was gunning for the coven, but other than stalking Tempest and dropping threatening fascist amulets, I'm still not sure how. And was dropping shit at my booth just a little nasty opportunity? What's his magic plan?"

She turned toward Lilith, and the man sitting next to her. His name was Azrael or something. She swore, everyone in Portland subcultures had some weird taken name. It was hard to keep track. And she knew that made her sound like her mother, but sometimes her mother was right, you know?

"ASP has never heard of this guy?"

They both shook their heads.

Azrael, a small white guy with a tattooed neck peeking out of his long-sleeved black T-shirt shook his head. His T-shirt had the ASP logo: the red pitchfork facing down in the classic three arrows anti-fascist symbol. The circle around the arrows was a red snake. An asp, she supposed. She hadn't noticed it on Daniel's T-shirt the other night.

"These libertarian Satanists want nothing to do with us, for obvious reasons, and we don't know everyone in the city," Azrael said.

"But there aren't that many Satanists of any stripe walking around," Lilith chimed in. Her facial piercings winked in the golden light. "But fascist theistic Satanists do exist...." She frowned. "We just didn't think there were any of them in Portland."

"There was that one guy who harassed Occupy ICE," said a big guy named Duke. Duke had a well-groomed brown beard that reached almost to his chest. "I thought it was pretty weird at the time, to see a dude with an upside-down pentagram harassing a bunch of anarchists and old hippies, but we just chased him off. Only saw him the once."

Duke shrugged and went back to his pint of cider.

"The point is..." Daniel said, practically vibrating. He was clearly impatient with this whole conversation but trying to be a good anarchist and listen to his comrades. "What are we going to do about this chud?"

"Is there anything you can do about him?" Ruby asked. "Or the community? I'm not used to going after solo agents, but I'm also not used to solo agents going after me."

Lilith smiled a feral smile. It made Ruby shiver.

"You hit the nail on the head there, Ruby. We need to access his networks. You think he was here the night the Patriots rolled through, so we can check on that. And then there's the Downtown Business Association, right? Those assholes hate us anyway. They helped campaign against our Satan in the Schools project."

"Which was part of the point," Azrael interjected.

"Indeed," Lilith replied. "Point is, this guy doesn't have much of a beef on his own."

"Except not getting hired by Brenda's shop," Daniel put in. "And Joshua's place, though we don't know that he's involved yet."

Lilith waved a hand, as if that was inconsequential. Ruby wasn't so sure. Guys like him? They took rejection personally.

"At any rate, I suggest we find his networks, expose what we can..." Lilith continued.

"And go from there," Daniel finished.

"And go from there." Lilith smiled and raised her glass for a toast.

Everyone followed suit, and a succession of clinks sounded around the table.

The Satanists were smiling, having decided on the next small course of action.

But Ruby still felt uneasy about it all. They were still missing something.

She just knew it.

27

TEMPEST

Raquel's living room was a warm refuge from the deepening cold outside.

A fire crackled on the hearth beneath the gorgeous painting of Raquel's son, Zion, when he was younger. Around five. It depicted the Tarot card The Sun, and his chubby little arms were flung out in glee. Tempest felt the disparity between the Summer Solstice feeling of that painting and the Winter Solstice reality she was sitting in. But at least she wasn't alone. The whole coven was here tonight.

Raquel bent over the fire. In addition to a long-burning, locally made wax-and-woodchips log, Raquel slowly added a few birch and cedar sticks that perfumed the air. She stood, brushing her hands off on her jeans, and tugged down the rust-orange sweater that made her dark skin glow.

"I wish Charlie was here," Raquel said. "I feel like this situation needs all hands on deck."

Charlie was Raquel's partner, a tall Viking of a man who ran the neighborhood game shop and bore an uncanny resemblance to movie Thor.

"Since there's magic involved, I just wanted to get this info to the coven first," Moss replied. A thin, geeky Japanese-American man with a faux hawk, tonight he wore his favorite gray knitted cowl and a forest-green sweater. He was the coven's most dedicated activist, and Tempest admired the hell out of him.

Raquel snorted. "When isn't there magic involved? I think our community—especially our partners—are pretty used to this shit by now."

Moss opened his mouth to object, but Raquel waved her hands to stop him. "Oh, I'm not disagreeing with you. I'm just pissed off that we're going to have another damn holiday ruined and I'd rather be with my sweetheart than in a meeting with you all."

"Gee, Raquel, I'm starting to think you don't love us anymore," Tobias quipped. His goatee was neatly trimmed, and tousled brown hair fell over his face, as usual. He sat on a big floor cushion at the base of the long red sofa where Tempest sat, flanked by Selene on one side and Moss on the other. Brenda took up the end. They were a little squished, but being surrounded by coven mates was calming Tempest down.

"So, you were saying this pendejo is the son of someone in the Downtown Business Association?" Lucy asked. Her work clothes were spattered with paint and she practically vibrated as she tugged her chocolate brown hair back into a ponytail. "Why the hell should he even care about us? I'm still not getting it. Are we a threat to his job prospects? Or his inheritance or something? Don't get me wrong, Moss, good job getting that intel, but I still don't see what to do with it."

Alejandro cleared his throat. He was in one of the club chairs arranged near the fire. Raquel took the other. The other coven members were either in chairs dragged in from the dining room or on floor cushions like Tobias. Alejandro wore pristine dark wash jeans, and a lavender dress shirt peeked out from beneath a clearly expensive black cashmere sweater that complemented his silver-shot black hair. He was always the best-dressed member of the coven.

"If he's threatening us because of the business association, clearly it benefits him somehow. Or maybe he's just a daddy's boy and anyone who messes with Daddy messes with him." Alejandro leaned forward, forearms resting on his knees. "Here's the thing I don't get: the coven has never attacked the downtown association directly. We've done a few things that have pissed them off, sure, but we've never come after *them*. That makes me suspect something else is going on."

"Do you have any ideas?" Lucy asked. "Because, except for Tempest's visions, I have no idea how to even approach this. Plus, someone attacked your wards, right?" Lucy had turned her dark eyes toward Tempest.

Tempest nodded, and cupped the back of her neck with her hand. It ached a little tonight. The feeling of the breached ward in her aura still lingered, even though Brenda and Raquel had both assured her that her boundaries looked solid.

"It could just be a personal beef, right?" Tobias said. "Because Brenda and Joshua rejected him as a reader? And that would make sense of his attacks on Ruby, too. First, she's antifascist, and second, she dissed him directly at the craft fair."

Tempest stared into the fire, breathing into her center. She was listening to the conversation but didn't have anything to add. Her spirit felt restless, despite Selene's calming energy. The flames danced and snapped, shades of pale yellow and deep orange. Her eyes kept returning to the glowing red and black embers at the base of the fire. There was something there...

"And then the amulet at the shop. That's another shot fired, right?" Lucy looked around. No one spoke, though a few people nodded. "So, we have enough information to counter him, magically. But I don't want to go on offensive until we have a clearer reason why he's doing this. Is it the personal beef? Is it related to the downtown association? Or is it a combination of the two? Not knowing will mess with any offensive magic. Defense, we can do."

"But that's not going to be enough," Raquel said, hands cradling a mug of tea. She took a thoughtful sip.

"Right. Not going to be enough. At least, that's the sense I get," Lucy replied.

"Tempest?"

She ripped her gaze from the fireplace and looked back at Lucy. Then at Brenda and Raquel. Selene gave her leg a quick squeeze of support.

Tempest shook her head, then exhaled. She looked back into the flames, and at those embers burning at the base of the fire. The wood coals were packed tightly, and the fire burned hot. The flames near the red and black embers burned blue and white. There was something....but what was it?

"Stay with it," Brenda's voice said, softly. "Drop into it. Let your body relax."

Tempest slowed her breathing down. In. Pause. Out. Pause. In. Slow and steady. With each inhalation she breathed into her center, and as she exhaled, she let herself relax and deepen into the liminal state she'd been practicing to increase her clairvoyance.

Breathe in the embers. Breathe out the fire. Breathe in the embers. Breathe out the fire.

Breathe in...

The air around her grew stifling. Choking. The smoke tasted acrid on the back of her tongue. She remembered the fires from a year ago. The ones burning in the city. The ones the coven helped put out. She saw visions of that night, when the mayor shook that developer's hand, people surrounding him on the concrete steps as news cameras filmed.

And the coven had struck, quenching the fires. But some of the embers still burned.

"The mayor. We tried, but we never took care of the mayor."

What else was there? Her spirit sought out the messages held within the crackling flames, the steady embers.

"At the base of the fires we put out, the embers still burn, banked against the future. Banked. Against the future. Banked."

Her tongue felt heavy in her mouth. Her eyelids flickered, opened and closed. Opened and closed. Her breath. Her heartbeat. All. So. Slow.

"The. Embers..." The vision from that night swirled around her, though she hadn't even been there. The images were fed from the minds of those who were. The coven. Arrow and Crescent. Forming one body and one mind. This thing they built together. The coven egregore.

Picture after picture flashed into her mind. Snapshots. And there. Then gone. *Wait!* She tried to call the image back. Scroll through.

But her body grew tired. She needed a break. The pressure was too great.

Diana, help me. One simple prayer to the Goddess of the hunt. The protector of children. The healer of mothers.

A trickle of energy flowed into Tempest. She had some vague awareness of Moss's hand on her back, and Selene's hand on her knee. Someone in the room was humming.

Her eyes flickered back open. *Show me the thing I need to see.* With heavy eyelids, she forced herself to gaze back into the fire. At those embers, black and red. Glowing. Fissures. Cracks. Like lava bubbling up from the dark earth.

"I need to see!" Her voice rasped. The humming sound increased.

And an image. Two faces, standing at the back of the crowd of suits and coats, standing on concrete steps.

Two white men, faces glowing in the lights of the cameras, standing just at the edges of a group of other, clearly powerful, men. Two men who looked alike.

Her stalker.

And his father.

"They were there. That night at the press conference when the coven took the developer down. They were there."

The humming stopped. The vision broke. Tempest collapsed back onto the couch.

Firm cushions. Soft hands.

Just breathe, the thought came. And, with a shuddering inhalation, her body remembered how.

28

RUBY

The people who could stay split into two workgroups at either end of the table. Ruby and Daniel sat next to one another on the long bench against the pub wall, fresh cider and some snacks in front of them. Lilith, Azrael, and Duke were at the other. Lilith had dragged a laptop out of her pack and was busy. Ruby could see what looked like a million tabs open on her browser already, and they'd only been at it for ten minutes. Lilith was the only one with an actual computer. Everyone else did searches bent over their phones.

The music had switched to a local ska band and the darts game had grown raucous. A group of anarchists had shown up and were crowded in the bar. Usually they'd be out at the courtyard tables, smoking, eating falafel from the food truck, and talking smack. But hardy souls that they were, she guessed sitting out in the snow was too much even for them.

Ruby chewed on a piece of salami. She wasn't hungry, but the snack was good, anyway. Plus, it would soak up some of the alcohol. Ruby liked her drinks, but had ordered a glass instead of a pint, and was glad of it. She needed a clear head and didn't have Daniel's tolerance for the booze.

Ruby knew this research needed to get done, but the timing still felt bad. She really needed to be working on getting her business shit taken care of, not spending her time chasing down a chud, as Daniel had called the guy.

It didn't matter how cute Tempest was; if Ruby didn't figure out how to make her business more profitable, she needed to seriously rethink her strategies. But this was in front of her right now. Right?

So, go with it, Rubes. You can worry about Woven Magic later. Besides, the chud had attacked her business, hadn't he? She bent her head back to her phone and scrolled through the business association website one more time, looking for any clues. The trouble was, she didn't know what, exactly, they were all looking for, because the guy didn't seem to be an actual member of the association, so why this weird beef?

And why had he targeted Ruby? Was it just random, because she'd told him to get lost?

But...seriously? "Who carries those kind of amulets around?"

Daniel looked up. "What's that?"

"The chud. Brad. He didn't come to Geeks and Bells aiming to put the whammy on me. Or I don't think he did. Right? I mean, what are the odds that he saw me here the other night—if he's with the Patriots—and tracked me down?"

Daniel nodded. "His attack on you seemed opportunist, because you pissed him off. Now that he knows you're associated with Tempest, though? He might target you again."

She took a couple sips of crisp cider, thinking.

"But that's the thing. I mean, I don't know anything

about magic." She waved a hand. "But why the hell would anyone just happen to have a bunch of amulets in their pocket?"

Daniel set his own pint down. "And charged-up amulets, too. That's a good point."

"I still don't get the 'charged-up' thing, either."

"It just means he has done some sort of ritual to imbue the amulets with his intention. They've got more juice in them than when he bought them or had them made."

"Okay. Makes sense, I guess."

"It doesn't matter if you believe in it, Rubes. What matters is that he believes in it."

"Beliefs make people dangerous," Azrael quipped.

She nodded, then picked up a cracker and another hunk of cured meat, stacking them together. "Kind of like I have to believe my character has certain powers in order to make the RPG stay interesting."

"Close enough," Daniel replied. "But like Azrael said, a lot more dangerous than interesting. Clearly the guy has some belief system he's working with that includes the need to attack people he sees as a threat."

"But that leads me back to my question. Why would someone ritually charge up a stack of amulets and carry them around?"

Daniel leaned back against the wall and picked up his pint. Ruby took another bite of cracker and salami.

"That's a very good question." He turned on the bench, so he could face her. She swiveled, too. His face was serious, brow furrowed, mind clearly working on a problem. "I'm so used to the magic stuff, I didn't even think to question that. It means he's been planning this for quite some time. Right? Because he had to get the amulets. Cleanse them. Do whatever workings he had to do to charge them. Every step of that kind of magic takes time."

"So, what's he doing? And why? Any clue?"

Lilith's voice broke through their little bubble. "I've got something!"

"Really?"

Ruby and Daniel scooted off the bench and walked over to the clump of Satanists. Lilith sat on the end of the bench, wall side, with Azrael next to her. She shoved her laptop to the center of the table. Duke stood and joined Ruby and Daniel so they could all face Lilith's screen.

And there, large as life, was a photo of the chud, blond sweep of hair falling across his forehead, what had to be that damn upside-down pentagram winking from beneath the open collar of his shirt. He was shaking hands with the mayor.

"Remember that big scandal a year or so ago? That developer the mayor was in bed with? Well, dear old Brad and his father have shares in the real estate investment company that funded that developer. It's a consortium of private funders and VCs."

Lilith took the computer back and tapped in some more info. A new screen appeared.

"And six months ago, Brad started the Merovingian Trust. Daddy is on the board. And guess who's a board advisor?" Lilith stretched her neck. "Can you all sit back down? Craning my neck is killing me."

"Who's a board advisor?" Duke asked.

"The mayor."

"No way!" Daniel said, as he went to grab their drinks from the other end of the long table. "Also, fucking Merovingian. Could he be any more blatant?" Daniel said,

"I don't get it." Ruby felt like that was her response to this whole situation. She was getting tired of it.

Ruby slid back onto the outside bench next to Duke. Lilith pulled her laptop close again and clicked some keys.

Daniel set Ruby's glass of cider down and slid in next to her. "Short form? They were a Frankish dynasty. The Nazis thought the Black Sun symbol came from the Merovingians."

"Thanks," she said. But she still felt confused.

"I was running searches on all the members of the downtown association and found a pic from one of those big charity events rich people like to dress up for," Lilith said.

"Philanthropists," Daniel snorted. "They can't just give their money away without a bunch of fuss, can they?"

Lilith raised a well-groomed eyebrow.

"Sorry," Daniel said. "Go on."

"Anyway. I saw our guy next to old Martin, here. And in the same group was the mayor, the developer, and the guy that works to fund all the private prisons in the Pacific Northwest. Plus, look at what Brad is wearing."

"No. Shit." Azrael said.

Lilith turned the computer so the three on the opposite bench could see. It was a zoomed-in section of a photo, a bit pixelated. It looked like someone's suit, with a long, black tie slicing down the center of a burgundy shirt. Over that was some fancy, angular silver pendant, with some sort of fancy scrollwork at the bottom.

Lilith clicked, and the photo zoomed out to regular size. And yep, there he was, the chud. Standing next to the guy that looked an awful lot like him. Dear old Dad. But...

Ruby shook her head. "I don't get it. What is that symbol?"

Daniel laughed. "You've seen it before, Rubes."

"I have?"

He pulled out his black knit cap and showed her the folded-up edge. She ran her fingers over the black watch cap and traced the black embroidery there. Sure enough, it was the same symbol.

"I never noticed it before, because of the black on black. It doesn't stand out."

"Unless you know what you're looking for," Duke replied.

"So, what is it?"

"It's the sigil of Lucifer. If Satan is the Challenger, then Lucifer is the Liberator. And frankly, it pisses me off that this guy is wearing that sigil. The inverted pentagram is bad enough."

"Why does that piss you off? I mean, I get that he's not your kind of Satanist, but..."

Daniel's mouth set in a line.

"Because, assholes like him don't get that the Light-bearer is supposed to liberate all consciousness. Free all people. Assholes like him think it's only about their own ego. As long as *they're* free, they don't give a shit about anyone else."

"I don't get it, though," Azrael chimed in. "Why does Martin here let his son gallivant around in Satanic jewelry?"

"That's the truly evil thing," Lilith smirked. "Dear old Dad seems to think it makes him look religiously tolerant. And he uses that to his fucked-up advantage."

"How?" Ruby asked. This was all so damn confusing.

"He uses his son as some sort of religious diversity fill quotient. So he can avoid hiring Muslims."

"What the fuck?" Azrael's voice dripped with disgust.

Lilith shrugged. "I don't really get it either, but so far, my research says he's been making it work for him."

"Anarcho-capitalists like pretending they're all badass. I bet associating with a known Satanist makes them think they're living on the edge." Duke said.

And Ruby felt completely over her head.

None of this explained all of those charged-up amulets.

Or why the chud was targeting her.

29

TEMPEST

Tempest sat cross-legged on the couch. Moss had shifted to a floor cushion perched at the base of Alejandro's chair to give her more space.. Tobias stood behind her, hands at her temples, doing some energy work that staved off the massive headache that had spiked through her a few seconds after she dropped out of her vision trance.

Heat seeped into her hands from the heavy ceramic mug Brenda had pressed on her a few minutes ago. The mug felt good. Her fingers moved lightly from rough texture to smooth. She knew the glaze shaded from rust to green and blue. One of Raquel's collection of hand thrown mugs. The chamomile tea was still too hot to drink, but it smelled good. Soothing. Grassy.

"So..." She cleared her throat.

"Tea should be cool enough if you need it," Brenda said.

Tempest took an experimental sip. It was. Just. She opened her eyes and blinked. Raquel poked at the fire. Moss tapped at his phone, occasionally pausing to show something to Alejandro, who grimaced. Lucy's eyes were closed. She got up early for work.

Cassiel looked at her expectantly from her dining room chair. And Selene still sat, steady and soothing, at Tempest's side.

Coven. Family.

No matter what happens, remember that, she told herself.

No matter what happened, she had to hold onto that sense of home. It was always the first thing to crumble inside her. But she'd been learning how to fight.

Brenda nodded, as if she'd heard her thoughts. "You were saying?"

"So, did you all see that? What I was seeing?"

Raquel closed the fire screen, which Tempest was grateful for. She didn't need another trip into the flames. She sat back down and picked up her own mug of tea from the low coffee table in the center of the room.

"I did," she said. "And I could feel other people feeding you images from that night, once they started to flow. But I couldn't see whatever that last image was that took you out."

"It was the whole thing that took me out," Tempest replied. "I'm only a little bit better than I was. My body's not strong enough yet."

Tobias's voice came from behind her and he switched his healer's hands to her shoulders. "Healing is a process. You've been sick for years, along with the PTSD from your childhood, Tempest."

"I don't have..." she started to interject, but Tobias talked right over her.

"It's going to take time to feel better. For your energy to increase."

"And it seems to me you were plenty strong enough."

Raquel fixed her gaze on Tempest, as if challenging her to disagree.

Tempest just shrugged beneath Tobias's hands.

"No. Don't shrug. Part of being a witch is taking responsibility for our actions and contributions, both good and bad."

"It's called pride," Selene murmured. "It's one of the marks of a witch."

Tempest squirmed inside, chest and belly tight with shame.

Goddess. Shame? Really? She felt disgusted with herself for that. She should know better by now.

"Don't do that," Brenda said. "Don't tie yourself up inside. Raquel and Selene are right. You did well tonight. And that is something to be proud of. Breathe that in for a moment, and then tell us what you saw."

Tempest did as her mentor told her and struggled to take in another deep breath. It helped.

"Now, exhale and expand your aura," Tobias said. "Start with your ætheric body and move outward."

She did, and felt her edges relax and stabilize again. The tension in her belly loosened. It worked. It almost always did.

"Okay. Tobias, I think I'm ready. Thanks."

He removed his hands, but the energy still moved through her. It felt good. She waited until he was back on his cushion with his own cup of tea. Moss and Alejandro stopped whatever it was they were doing, and Lucy had opened her eyes. They all waited. For her. As if she was in the lead.

That was something she hadn't felt before. She tested the feeling, poking at it as if poking at a sore tooth, only to find that the soreness was gone. Huh.

She drank more tea and spoke.

"I saw my stalker. Nazi Guy or whatever we're calling him. On the steps, that night Cassie and Joe and the rest of you took that developer down. My eyes kept going back to the coals. The embers. We put out the fire, but the embers were still banked."

"Banked against the future, you said." Lucy sat forward in her chair.

"Yeah. We didn't finish it. The whole situation was just waiting."

"To bite us in the ass again," Moss said.

"Here's the thing: Nazi Guy was standing back, barely lit by those camera lights, and next to him was an older man in a fancy tan overcoat. And he looked just like the asshole. Same jawline. Same eyes."

"That's because it's his father, Martin," Moss replied, holding up his phone and waggling it back and forth. "Ruby and Daniel did a bunch of research tonight. They met with some members of ASP, too." He glanced down at his phone. "Martin and Brad Chadwick both worked with the investment company that funded that asshole developer. And looks like baby Brad has a new company. The Merovingian Trust."

"Oh great. That's just what we need. A white nationalist trust in white nationalist–riddled Oregon."

"I've met Martin Chadwick. He's an ass, but I always thought he was second string. He never struck me as a power player. I'll be damned," Raquel said, then looked up. "Just kidding, Yemoja. Don't want to be damned."

A lightbulb lit in Tempest's head.

"But that's what he's trying to do," she said. "Brad Chadwick. It feels like he's using everything within his power to damn us all."

"Well, fuck him," Moss said. "Whatever changed to make this loser a force in the city? We're a force, too. We can give as good as we get."

That's what Tempest was afraid of.

30

RUBY

Ruby had finally taken a shower and gotten dressed. She was in the kitchen, heating up some lunch. As she stirred the thick vegetable stew, her brain kept worrying at Woven Magic's cash flow issues.

The gas range needed cleaning, she noticed. And so did the hood. She and her housemates were pretty good at keeping common spaces clean.

Ruby headed to the sink to wash out the glass container the stew had come in. She stared out the streaky glass of the window above the sink. Outside, the clouds were almost black. It looked like more snow was on the way. The holly tree in a neighboring yard crouched beneath a towering Douglas fir. Its glossy dark green leaves and bright red berries reminded Ruby of how much her grandmother had loved this season, and holly in particular.

As the warm, soapy water sluiced over her hands, her thoughts returned to her morning's work. Her finances were definitely a wreck, but not quite as bad as she feared. She'd actually made more money than she'd thought at first. Maybe a good accountant could actually sort her out.

She should talk with Sean and Carla. Brainstorm about a new business plan. And meanwhile, maybe a part-time job to get her through the next six months wasn't such a bad idea.

Wiping her hands on a burgundy tea towel, she sniffed the air. The stew smelled warm and ready, which was good, because she'd skipped breakfast.

Her phone buzzed. She looked down. Tempest.

"Sometimes you need a break to look at the big picture. Get out from the weeds," Desi said.

"Huh." Tempest was cancelling. Or, not exactly cancelling, but changing plans. She wanted to invite Daniel and Lawrence along on their date. Which meant it wasn't going to be a date. Ruby's heart sank. Damn it. Why were women so weird?

She punched a question back with her thumbs.

I'm sorry. I still want a date. Just not tonight.

She texted back. *I still don't understand. Are you brushing me off, or what?*

The bubbles on her screen showed that Tempest was typing. Ruby just stood there in the kitchen, lunch forgotten, waiting.

No. But things are escalating. I think we're running out of time. Daniel and Lawrence are coming by. Can you still come?

Well, shit. So much for a pleasant evening, getting to know someone new.

Sure, Ruby texted back.

Damn it. She tapped out a message to Sean.

I need your help. Carla's too.

What's up? came the reply.

More Nazi stuff, she typed in. *And if there's time, business, too.*

There was a long pause. Ruby filled a white ceramic

bowl with fragrant stew and headed to the table. Her phone buzzed with the incoming text.

We're in. Just let us know what time.

31

TEMPEST

Tempest dragged around the shop, brain in a serious fog, wanting nothing more than to curl up in one of the chairs in the reading area and take a nap. She'd taken her CBD oil this morning, along with her other meds, but it wasn't enough. Not after the energy expenditure of the last few days.

Alexander James Adams's guitar filled the shop with yuletide songs. His melodic voice was a comfort to Tempest, and she needed it. Life was seriously just too much right now.

Plus, she felt bad about cancelling her date with Ruby. But there was too much weirdness flying around for her to focus on anything but the Solstice and the magic the coven was going to need to do.

Besides, if Ruby couldn't hang with this, maybe she wasn't the woman for Tempest after all.

As if that's fair.

So, it was an excuse. So what? Tempest really did need more time. She had way too much on her plate and not enough spoons to deal with it.

She wiped down glass and wood countertops with a soft cloth and Brenda's favorite natural cleaning spray. It helped keep the dust down, and besides, the task felt soothing. She needed soothing.

Tempest always told her clients the same things Tobias told her. Healing was a process. It came in fits and starts. Just because she was improving, didn't mean she could just go out and run the magical equivalent of a marathon.

Her body needed to work up to it. Get stronger.

Her head knew that, but she was sick of it. Chronic illness was so damn frustrating, especially when she did all the right things. Meds. Rest. Avoiding inflammatory foods. Taking herbs. Meditating.

Her condition especially stung because she was a healer, at a loss for how to help herself.

She picked up a statue of Freya and wiped it down before moving on to the others in the Norse pantheon. Next table over were statues representing the Greek and Roman Gods. She started with Apollo, leaving Diana for last.

Diana held pride of place in the display today, on a plexi riser in the center of the glass table, bow pointing toward a stained-glass crescent moon in the front window. Tempest smiled. Almost no one noticed where Diana was aiming.

"Always shoot for the moon," Tempest murmured. Not that she felt up for it today. Today, everything just felt hard.

Tempest ran the cloth over Diana's bow. At least she didn't still have school on top of everything else.

People expected their healers to be in full health at all times. As if they weren't allowed any flaws. As if being sick didn't give her special insight into people's bodies. Healthy, physically powerful people didn't know shit about the healing process, because they didn't have to.

But the slight tang of shame remained.

"Tempest, are you okay?"

She looked up to see Brenda looking at her with concern. The purple curtain that led to the back of the shop rippled. Her mentor held a pile of bright altar cloths in her arms, ready for pricing and display.

"I'm just exhausted. The past few days have been...too much."

She'd been about to say they'd sucked, but that wasn't one-hundred-percent true. It seemed as though her psychic skills were increasing, for one thing. And considering how hard she'd worked on them, that was good.

Plus, stressful as the week had been, she'd met Ruby.

"Do you need to go home? We should be slow until this afternoon."

"The store needs restocking, and you need help with that." That was always the case during the Yule season. There was always work to be done at the Inner Eye, customers or not.

Brenda set the stack of bright cloth down on the main counter, near the cash point, clearly worried.

That was another thing about being chronically ill: people worried about you all the time. The smallest thing could make her friends want to send her back to bed or offer her another damn herbal tea.

The bells on the door jangled and in walked Joshua, wearing a long red wool coat and a black wool top hat. Even in the dead of winter, her landlord was a dandy, through and through.

"Joshua!" Brenda said, heading toward him with a smile. "What brings you out of your shop?"

The two embraced, then stepped apart. Joshua came toward Tempest, arms out.

"How are you feeling?" he asked as he enfolded her in arms that smelled of wool, ambergris, and cold.

"Been better," she replied.

Brenda was back behind the long glass counter, so Joshua headed there, unbuttoning the long swoop of a coat. Tempest followed, setting down her dust cloth.

"I'm here because I got a little gift this morning."

He pulled a black velvet bag from one coat pocket and set it on the counter with a dull clank.

Tempest grew very still. She could almost feel the badness emanating from behind the velvet.

"Another one?" Brenda asked.

Joshua nodded, then swept his top hat off, took off his gloves, and ran his fingers through his dark hair. He set the hat on the counter, top down.

"Found it above the back door this morning, along with a note."

He dragged a small slip of white paper from the bag, fingers careful not to touch the amulet inside.

Smoothing it on the counter, he turned it with long fingers so Brenda and Tempest could read it.

"'Welcome to the end of days, asshole. Enjoy the left - hand turn,'" Brenda read out loud. "A bit melodramatic, but that doesn't sound good, all the same."

A shiver walked up Tempest's spine. She hated seeing the amulet inside the boundaries and wards of the shop. She knew Joshua and Brenda would take care of it, neutralize its power, but it shouldn't be here.

"Enjoy the left-hand-turn. What does that mean?" she asked.

"It could mean anything," Joshua replied. "But since this Nazi fool is working with the Black Sun and we're coming up on Solstice? He's planning some nasty magic to counter the returning of the sun. Some Ragnarok bullshit."

His words felt as true as Diana's arrows. Tempest felt them in her bones.

"What's my part in all of this?" she asked, barely aware she'd said the words aloud.

Joshua laid a gentle hand on her wrist. "For some reason, Tempest, things seem to be circling around you. How's that crack in your aura? May I look?"

She nodded, feeling a strange tingling sensation as he did a psychic scan.

He and Brenda exchanged a look.

"You mostly seem okay," he said, "but there's a slight impression still, and I can't tell if it's just a seam healing itself up, or if it's a vestige of someone else's power. And seeing as he's the only one who seems to be attacking right now, it makes sense that the ward breach came from him."

"Brenda?" Tempest looked at her mentor, whose eyes traced an area a foot around Tempest's body, face troubled.

"I think he's right. And that seam looks...wrong. I'm so sorry we didn't notice it before."

Tempest's voice trembled. "Can you get it out?"

Brenda started to say, "Of course," just as Joshua held out a hand and said, "No!"

Their voices clashed in the shop, discordant above the music that still played on, calm and cheerful as you please. Tempest's stomach lurched and a headache gathered at the base of her skull.

"We can use the connection," Joshua said, then looked at Tempest with serious, intense eyes. "If you're willing to, that is. We can use his connection to you to direct the magic. Hopefully stop whatever messed-up ritual he's planning. Take him down."

Tempest wanted to crawl back into bed with Graymalkin and sleep until Christmas day.

"I don't think I can," she said. "I'm so tired. I just…"

Brenda slid her hands to the back of Tempest's neck and began massaging her tightly corded muscles.

"We'll help you, Tempest. We'll be with you all the way," Joshua was saying.

"But it's still your choice," Brenda replied. "You're the boss of your own soul."

But what was the *right* choice? Figuring out the answer felt like too heavy a burden to bear.

32

RUBY

Ruby took the bus back to Hawthorne again. Her hatchback was all-wheel drive, but since she was only carrying herself, not having to deal with other drivers seemed like a good bet in the weird, intermittent snow.

The street was busy with people heading to the grocery store or out to dinner after work, happy faces shining beneath the festive holiday lights. Cars moved past in a steady stream, most of them coming from the direction of the bridge. People going home to neighborhoods where transit was a too-many-transfers pain in the ass.

Her boots treads slipped on a patch of ice. Arms out, she caught herself before falling. She paused, panting slightly, feeling a slight hitch in her lower back. Not too bad. She had worse back issues after a full weekend working a con.

It was the one problem with Portland snow when it showed up. She loved it, and it lasted just the right length of time, but it also came in fits and starts, meaning it had time to melt and refreeze, forming a layer of treachery beneath a fresh fall of pretty white.

She turned up a side street before hitting Cesar Chavez,

heading toward Tempest's place. Both Daniel and Lawrence had decided it was a security risk to hold another meeting in an unknown, public space. If Liberation Cider House wasn't closed on Monday nights, they would have met up there.

Why they thought Tempest's place would be safe since she was one of the objects of attack, Ruby didn't know.

She huffed out in annoyance, breath steaming white in the cold, dark air. The side streets up here were relatively quiet, and usually a little dark for Ruby's liking. But this time of year, there were twinkle lights everywhere, strung from porches and in the bare branches of the trees that reached out overhead.

At least the brainstorming session with Sean and Carla had gone well. They'd both had a lot of good ideas, some of which she was kicking herself for not thinking of before. For the first time in a couple of months, Ruby felt hopeful about her business again.

Now if she could only make some of the ideas work, and make Woven Magic more viable...

They'd also spent some time talking about Nazi Brad. Carla reminded them that, magic or not, the dude had stalked someone and threatened her friends. In a town where the Patriots regularly beat the shit out of people, they had to treat it as a credible threat.

Sean was all in to kick some Nazi ass if it came to it, and both of them seemed open to being part of some antifascist action, or even ritual, if it came to that. Seemed like everyone around her had been quicker to get on the magic-as-possible-useful-technology than she had been.

But at least she was on board, now. Mostly. Didn't mean a geeky Asian girl from Portland didn't still have questions, but diversity of tactics, right?

Tempest's place should be around here somewhere.

Ruby pulled her phone from her coat pocket and checked the address. Yep. The Craftsman with white lights around the porch, just up ahead. Nice looking place. Tempest lived in the garage apartment or something, so Ruby turned up the drive. Sure enough, the garage was double height, with stairs to one side. Lights glowed warmly from the front windows.

She clomped up the sturdy wooden stairs—lower back hitching just a bit—and rapped on the red Craftsman style door. The windowpanes were leaded, distorting her view of what was inside. Must be an antique door fitted to the new construction.

The door opened, and there she was, eyes huge, wearing tiny black jeans and gray slippers. The rest of her swam in a yellow hoodie that had to be three sizes too big. Tempest ducked her head a moment and backed up, opening the door even wider.

"Come in."

Ruby wiped her feet, then stepped inside onto a second mat. She bent to unlace her boots, toeing them off and setting them neatly next to the door.

"There's a hook for your coat. And your hat, if you want." Tempest pointed to the wall beside the door.

A gray cat stalked over, sniffed, then stalked away again.

"That's Graymalkin," Tempest said.

Once the whole ritual of arriving somewhere in the middle of an Oregon winter was over, red hat still on, Ruby just stood there in her stockinged feet, looking at Tempest.

"Hi."

"Hi," Tempest replied. "Look, I'm sorry about tonight. But I just..."

The poor thing looked as if she wished the wood floor would swallow her.

"It's okay. I get it. We all have a lot of things going on." Letting her off the hook. The words were mostly the truth, and even though Tempest's earlier texts had felt like rejection, looking at the woman now, Ruby just couldn't feel mad. Tempest was so obviously mortified.

Ruby was beginning to think she always was. Tempest alternated between seeming fierce and scared of her own shadow. Maybe dating her wasn't such a good idea after all. Maybe it would be too hard.

She still wanted to tuck a hand behind Tempest's delicate neck and kiss those sweet, pale lips, though. Her attraction wasn't going away, that was for sure.

"Do you want some tea? The kettle's on. Or I've got beer in the fridge."

Tempest walked over the mini kitchen area. Ruby followed, looking around as she went. The space felt nice. Cozy. Tempest had arranged the open space into zones. There was a bedroom area, a sitting area with a blue loveseat with a teal blanket thrown across the back and a battered, dark brown chair with a matching ottoman. Low bookcases ran along the far wall, beneath the window covered in heavy navy drapes.

The kitchen space was efficient. If Ruby didn't like her housemates so much, she could really dig living in a place like this.

She watched as Tempest went through the ritual of making tea. Rinsing out a pot. Shaking loose leaves and what looked like dried flowers into a strainer.

"Can you grab the mugs?" Tempest tilted her sharp little chin toward two mismatched thrift store mugs on the counter and followed her back to the seating area. Tempest set the pot on a small coffee table in front of the loveseat. Ruby set the mugs down, catching a whiff of the floral tea—

rose and something else—and Tempest. She smelled good, like warm girl and peppermint. It was all Ruby could do to not lick the ear peeking out from the short, platinum-blond hair.

Down girl. She canceled your date, remember? She's probably not even into you.

The way Tempest sighed and moved a little closer to Ruby before practically flinging herself backward and into the big chair made Ruby think that might not be right.

"Am I early?" Ruby asked.

"No. Daniel and Lawrence texted right before you got here. They missed their bus. Should be here soon."

Ruby crouched in front of the bookcases, eyes scanning the shelves. Some fantasy and science fiction novels. Couple of poetry books. And a bunch of books on magic. There were also small objects. Rocks. A small vase. A carved wooden box.

The top of the case directly beneath the window held what couldn't be a random display. The objects were too specific. A knife. A hand thrown ceramic cup. A shell. Some sort of incense burner.

And, surprisingly enough, what looked like a little dish of table salt.

Must be an altar of some sort.

"Tea's ready." Tempest's voice cracked a little on the first syllable. Yeah, she was definitely nervous.

Ruby sat on the loveseat and took the mug from Tempest's hands. The tea smelled like toasted rice. "What tea is this?"

"Gen mai cha. It's one of my favorites."

Ruby blew across the surface and took a tiny sip. Hot. But good. It had a roasted, nutty flavor. But she hadn't come here to talk about tea.

Tempest perched on the other end of the loveseat, looking as if she might bolt.

"You don't have to go on a date with me, you know."

Tempest looked up, startled, eyes as huge as a baby deer's. A red flush crawled up from the neck of the huge hoodie, staining her pale skin.

"I...it's not that...it's..."

"It's what?" Ruby kept her voice calm. Light. God, the girl was skittish.

"You make me nervous."

Ruby laughed, then settled back into the loveseat. Tempest was staring at her, a strange look on her face.

"Look," Ruby said, "I get it. I can be a bit much for people sometimes. But I'm still interested in you if you decide you want to go there. It's just a date, not a death sentence."

33

TEMPEST

"I know," Tempest replied, finally sitting back, cross-legged, in the loveseat. Graymalkin leapt up, taking advantage of her lap. After some minor adjustments, he settled in and closed his eyes.

How was Tempest supposed to explain that the problem was all in her own head? And body. And heart. She stroked Gray's silky fur and he began to purr.

Ruby sat across from her, black sweater and tight black jeans hugging her lush, wide, body. Those red lips were still smiling, though it was looking a little strained.

That smile waited for Tempest to say something. But what could she say? That she'd never had sex with anyone? That people looking at her the way Ruby looked at her made her want to crawl under a table and disappear?

Except...maybe that wasn't true. Because she also had the urge to crawl on Ruby's lap. Find out what those red lips tasted like.

"I'm just..." She looked down at her tea, then back up again. "I'm just really shy. And I don't know how to deal with all of this." She waved the hand that wasn't clutching the handle of her tea mug so hard she might crack it.

And like Goddess Diana I'm a virgin, even though my coven mates think that whole concept is bullshit and I need to stop thinking about sex as some weird, all-or-nothing event. Easy for them to say. They'd all had sex with actual people, and not just their own hands.

Ruby blinked, then took another sip of tea. "There is no 'all this,' Tempest. I'd just like a chance to get to know you, that's all."

They leaned toward each other, air crackling with tension.

I'm going to let this happen now, Tempest thought, and closed her eyes.

The sound of booted feet climbing her stairs penetrated her consciousness and Graymalkin leapt from her lap. The tension broken, Tempest's eyes snapped back open to find Ruby staring at her. Her eyes held a look Tempest couldn't identify.

But she liked it.

A rhythmic knock came at the door. Tempest set her mug down and stood, moving past the loveseat. Ruby placed a hand on her wrist, stopping her.

"Hey," she said, looking up at Tempest with those dark eyes, black hair framing her face beneath the red wool cap that matched her lips. "I don't want to scare you, Tempest. I'm into you, but whatever you decide is cool. Okay?"

Tempest nodded. Ruby's hand dropped from her wrist, and Tempest padded across the small space to the door.

She opened the door. Daniel and Lawrence just stood there, letting in the cold.

"Uh...guys? You coming in?"

Lawrence shook his head, the fake fur around the hood of his black, Army-style coat ruffling.

"You gotta see something first. Put on your boots."

"What's happening?" Ruby came up behind her.

Tempest slipped into her boots and, arms wrapped around herself, stepped onto the landing.

Daniel's gloved finger pointed to where the sturdy stair rail met the outside wall of her apartment. He scraped away a line of snow and Tempest saw it.

The dull gleam of pewter.

Her heart raced, and she flashed hot beneath her sweat-shirt despite the cold.

"Another one. Joshua just found one today, too."

"An amulet?" Ruby's voice came from inside the apartment. "Hey, guys? You better shut the door or come in. This cat is going nuts trying to get out."

"Let him," Tempest replied. There was a scrabbling sound, and within seconds, Graymalkin had leapt up on the thick railing and was sniffing at the edge of the amulet. He hissed, and then, mouth open wide, yowled. Tempest gathered him into her arms.

"We need to contain it," Daniel said.

"There are plastic tubs in one of the kitchen drawers," Tempest replied, face buried in Gray's fur. She couldn't take her eyes off of the seam in the wood and that dull, gunmetal gray line peeking out. "And salt in the cupboard."

She knew that much. To temporarily neutralize a spell, burying it in salt was as good a way as any.

She just wondered how long it would last.

34

RUBY

The spell was "neutralized," and a bunch of texts sent and phone calls had been made. As a result, Tempest's little apartment was crowded all of a sudden. The poor cat had retreated to the bed, where he was giving his paws a bath.

Joshua and Selene had arrived from down the driveway, and Moss had rolled up on a break from his gig job driving other folks around in the winter mess.

Moss had declared that the loveseat had room for his skinny ass, which was fine with Ruby. It meant that Tempest was snugged up against her in the middle. Ruby was trying to be cool about it, but it was hard to not be a total dog and put a hand on the witch's knee, or around her shoulder.

Down girl, she thought to herself, though the fact that Tempest smelled of toasted Japanese tea and warm girl wasn't helping.

She focused on the people crowded around her, sitting on chairs and cushions or on the wood floor.

Sean and Carla had showed after she texted, and Lilith, Azrael, and Duke responded to Daniel's call. They were all engaged in animated conversation and drinking tea, with the exception of Lilith, whose head was bent over her laptop, fingers poised to strike.

Ruby couldn't express how much seeing their faces meant to her. It wasn't that they'd shown up for her, because they hadn't. It was that... Community. All of these people had shown up for community.

She knew that Portland was rad, and that folks threw down for whoever was in need, but sometimes that felt theoretical. Like when she was struggling with her business and didn't have much time to show up herself. But at times like these it hit home that solidarity was real.

And if that was true, maybe this whole weird thing they were all planning could be pulled off.

Moss was talking, leaning forward, tea mug in one hand, orange T-shirt illustrated with little black dust sprites from *My Neighbor Totoro*. Ruby wondered why they hadn't spent more time together. He seemed cool, and it was clear he and Daniel hung out a fair bit.

"Brad and his father were at that press conference last year when we took out that crooked developer and implicated the mayor," Moss was saying.

Daniel snorted. "Not that anything ever happened to the mayor. That guy is Teflon, I swear."

Ruby set her mug down and began rooting in her backpack, drawing out a metal cylinder that had protected a bottle of fancy whiskey in its former life. Next, she pulled out a plastic bag filled with a tangle of pale cream wool.

"You need a drink for this?" Lawrence asked. "Not that I'm complaining."

Ruby shot him a look as she twisted off the lid and drew out her spindle, a wooden wand, with a flat disc—the whorl

—near the top. She'd picked it up at a fiber arts con and had been experimenting with it for the past year.

"Drop spindle," she said. "Keep talking. Sometimes it just helps me to work while I listen." She wrapped a piece of yarn around the wand and hooked it on a metal hook on top of the whorl. Then she separated out a hank of the creamy wool and fed it onto the leader yarn.

"At any rate, not only does he work for his dad, he was probably part of the whole mess that led to the insurance fires that developer was setting." Moss continued.

Lilith kept frantically tap-tap-tapping away.

"So, we have four amulets now," Joshua said. "That is so not good."

"Also…" Tempest squirmed a little next to Ruby, clearly uncomfortable, "Joshua and Brenda think when my wards got cracked it was him. And some of him was left behind."

"Fuck," Daniel said, turning to Ruby. "Remember how I thought you might be tagged? Turns out it's Tempest."

Whoa. Ruby had no idea what to say to that, so she just kept pulling on the hank of wool and feeding it onto the growing skein of yarn.

He turned back to Tempest. "I'm sorry this is happening to you. But we got your back. ASP will be there for whatever you need, and so will I."

Lawrence leaned forward. "I think this is going to be another massive action, Tempest. How can I help support you?"

Tempest shook her head. "I don't know, but tomorrow is Solstice Eve. If he's gonna try something big, magic wise, it's probably going to happen tomorrow night or on Solstice Day itself."

Lilith raked a hand through her hair and looked up, seeming almost bewildered that there were other people in the room. "The business association is having their big holiday party tomorrow night. Coincidence?"

"I think not!" Daniel replied. "And that's pretty damn interesting. Could be a chance for an impromptu action?"

"I think we should let them know that one of their members has a white nationalist son, and that Daddy and Mayor Patterson both have links to his new project," Moss said. "We could round up a bunch of folks for that, I bet."

"But what about the ritual?" Ruby blurted, stopping the spindle between her knees. "Or the magic, or whatever?"

Tempest turned her elfin face Ruby's way, those pale lips too close all of a sudden. The toasted-tea and clean-woman scents made Ruby want to bury her face in Tempest's neck beneath that giant yellow hoodie.

"The coven will take care of it," Tempest said. "Maybe time it for after the action."

Then, with her small fingers, Tempest squeezed Ruby's hand.

"But we'll need you there," she said. "We'll need you there to spin."

Ruby's throat grew dry. "Why? I don't get what fiber arts have to do with any of this."

Those big dark eyes were steady for once. Not flinching. Not looking away. Not shy.

"I don't exactly know yet," Tempest said. "But he did target you, so you're tied to this. But mostly, it's just a feeling that to make the magic that turns the sunwise wheel, we'll need as much skill and talent as possible."

"And you've got that, Ruby," Carla said. "If the witches need a spinner, you're it."

She was. And wasn't that the damndest thing? That the thing she loved more than anything, the creation of fiber and making something with it, was necessary for a thing this weird and this big?

This freaked her out more than dodging a Nazi's fist.

She picked up the empty whiskey can and shook it.

"*Is* there any whiskey in this apartment?" she asked, trying to lighten the mood.

No one laughed.

35

TEMPEST

The amulets...the information...the breach in her personal wards...

All of it swirled in the air like flakes of snow, not quite landing.

Tempest stared at the yarn spooling itself out from between Ruby's fingers. The wheel, turning. Sunwise. Strengthening. Making.

"Magic," Tempest said.

Ruby looked surprised. "This? It's just spinning. I still don't get exactly what you're talking about. People have been making yarn for thousands of years."

It was clear that Ruby was trying, but Tempest wasn't the best at explaining magic to non-magical people. She was too new at it herself.

"There's a reason people call what Tempest and I do 'the Craft' you know." Daniel's face lightened. "And you're the one who named your business Woven Magic."

Ruby scowled, and muttered "D&D reference..." but just kept on with the mesmerizing task of turning wool into yarn.

"It's what Tempest was trying to explain, though," Joshua said. He and Selene were snuggled up on the floor on a couple of throw pillows. Together, they looked like some sort of Goth postcard. "About why we need you at the ritual? You're primarily a weaver, right? You literally make cloth out of raw material, starting with the spinning. You link that to your creative intention and fashion something new. Something useful and beautiful. For magic workers, that's powerful stuff."

"Yeah, that," Tempest said, glad someone else was able to put what she knew into words.

Ruby looked at her with those chocolate-brown eyes and blinked, then shrugged. Her fingers were so nimble, and her body so used to the practice of spinning, she didn't even break rhythm, just kept drawing out the pale tuft of wool and winding it onto the spindle. Pinching and pulling, spinning and dropping, the wool turned into yarn.

Amazing.

"I guess," she finally said.

Lawrence interceded. "Witches and Pagans tune in to the wheel of the year, no matter where we live. The turning of the seasons, the rotation around the sun...all of it affects our magic."

"Just like it affects our lives," Selene added. "People hang up lights in the middle of the darkest part of the year to remind ourselves the turn is about to happen. The days won't always get darker. Instead, after Winter Solstice, they'll grow lighter again."

"How is that magic?" Ruby asked. "It's just the way things work."

"We sync up with the natural powers to boost our magic, that's all," Selene continued. "The more in alignment with what's happening around us, the easier it is to do magic."

Daniel drank some more tea, clearly thinking. "You know, I've been chasing down rumors about a thing—even had Lilith here do more research on it—but I wasn't sure it applied. But with all this talk of seasonal magic, and the sunwise turn, I think my intuition was right."

The edges of Tempest's aura started buzzing. Daniel's words penetrated, but she couldn't take her eyes off Ruby's spindle and her hands.

The wool spooled into yarn, faster and faster. Ruby wound it around the long, wand-like spindle, then, with a flick, got it spinning clockwise again. Spooling. Winding. Spinning.

Something was trying to come through. Tempest felt it in her body, and in her energy fields. The buzzing hum harmonized with the soft sound of the spindle and the wool.

Her eyes blinked, unfocused, then blinked again.

"That Ritual of Undoing thing?" Lilith asked. "Ragnarok on a Satanist stick?"

"What the fuck is that?" Moss asked, setting down his mug.

"Sounds pretentious as hell," Lawrence replied.

"It is. But in certain hands, with enough power built up?" Daniel said. "It can do some serious damage."

Spinning and falling. Spinning and falling. Winding and unwinding. Time and tide. Moon and sun. The wheel of the year. The cycles of the earth.

Cracks. Cracks in her aura. Cracks in the cycles. Cracks in what was whole.

Destruction with no creation.

An ending with no beginning.

"Stop!" Tempest said, flinging up her free hand. "Just stop!"

She set her mug down on the floor, then stood up. Slowly.

Everyone stared. Waiting. Ruby's dark wood spindle sat on her lap again, clutched in her strong fingers. Still. Quiet.

Tempest shook her head, trying to focus.

"We'd been thinking the attack was about the coven, but it's not, and all of the business association stuff, and the mayor...that makes it even more clear. It's about what Arrow and Crescent *represents*. About what all of you represent."

She began to pace, from the seating area to the door, and back again, weaving her way between people perched on cushions or sitting cross-legged on the floor. She stepped over Lilith's outstretched legs. For once, the woman's hands were still on her keyboard.

"Think about it." Tempest searched for the words as her feet wove a pattern around her tiny apartment. "To a certain sector of Portland, we represent community action coupled with magic. We've clearly been trying to help. So..."

"Take out one major source of help and it rocks the larger community," Sean rumbled. "Makes them less able to cope with outside attacks. We've seen that before."

"Right?" Tempest replied, thoughts racing. "It's just like my immune system. It lacks a key component of internal support, so it gets weaker and weaker, and falls prey to every outside attack, no matter how small. So, I think this rite of whatever...?"

"The Ritual of Undoing," Daniel said.

"Well, that's the opposite of what the Thelemites and you other magician-types talk about, isn't it? The Great Work."

Ruby looked really confused.

"Daniel or Lawrence, can you explain again?" Tempest

said. Daniel leaned toward Ruby as Tempest went to fill the kettle for more tea, just to have something to do.

"The Great Work is the work of self-possession. Becoming wholly ourselves, in full alignment with every part of our soul and therefore, with the cosmos. So we can step into our True Will and do the work we're really meant to do in the world."

Tempest turned. "Daniel is right. He's working against that."

"Collectively, and as individuals," Lawrence muttered. "He wants us divided inside and out."

"And he wants to sever us from the natural cycles of the sun. That's the thing I kept seeing when you were spinning, Ruby."

Tempest felt her confidence growing with her words. In the back of her mind, she heard the water coming to a boil. A new energy filled her. The energy of certainty in the face of chaotic dissolution.

"I kept seeing that we can use the natural turn of the wheel against him. The community, united, can save itself."

"El pueblo unido jamás será vencido," Lucy murmured.

"What's that mean?" Carla asked.

"The people united, will never be defeated," she replied. "It's from the socialist movement in Chile and became a global resistance anthem."

Lucy's words hung in the air. Then the kettle clicked. The water had boiled.

"Who wants more tea?" Tempest asked. This was going to be a long meeting, on the edge of the longest night of the year.

Across the room, Ruby was looking at her intensely, a dark lock of hair falling across one round cheek. And for the first time, Tempest looked right back.

Things were terrible, but her community was rallying and her heart felt truly brave for the first time in weeks. She felt so brave, if they weren't in a room packed tight with people, she could have kissed those bright red lips.

Almost.

36

RUBY

It was freezing outside, and soft flakes of snow fell in the darkening afternoon sky.

Ruby's hands were sweating despite the cold.

"You're still planning to be there tonight?" Ruby asked. She juggled her keys in one hand and had a packing blanket slung over the other arm.

Sean stood on the sidewalk, holding her big spinning wheel, waiting for her to unlock her hatchback. Carla stood a few feet away, beneath a big, bare sycamore whose branches were entwined with white twinkle lights. She held a pile of blankets to tuck around the big wheel to keep it from jostling too much and to insulate the wood from the freezing temperatures.

"We said we would, lass, and we will. No one threatens our friends or our city without us stepping up if we can."

The whole plan was a bit confusing. First, the coven and their allies were confronting Nazi Boy, his father—and hopefully the mayor—at the business association holiday party. Then ritual at Raquel's house? Seemed like a lot of running around, but Arrow and Crescent Coven had a reputation that they knew what they were about, so Ruby guessed she would trust.

Or keep trying to.

Ruby sighed. "How can you be so sure we're doing the right thing? Or that it's going to be effective?"

She heard Carla snort softly at that, but it was Sean who answered.

"We can never know the long-term consequences, Ruby. But we have to figure out what's right inside, and in our relationship with the world, and act from there."

"That's it?" Ruby said, tucking keys into her coat pocket and swinging the back door up. She spread the packing blanket out, then helped Sean ease the big wheel into the back of her car, careful not to bump or scrape it. He cursed as it clipped his knee, but caught it. Luckily, his arms were long as well as muscular.

It wasn't great to load the wheel this early, but Ruby had wanted to take advantage of Sean's help. The wheel should be safe enough swaddled in the car while she ran errands and grabbed a bite to eat.

Carla stepped forward and began tucking the other blankets around the beauty.

"That's it," he said, stepping back. "We do the best we can with the resources and information we have."

Ruby tucked the blankets more securely around her old friend. She'd spent time getting it in perfect running order, and now wondered why. Transporting the wheel meant she'd need to make adjustments once she got to Raquel's anyway.

You needed to tinker with your wheel because that's part of your deal, isn't it? Working with the tools of her craft and trade calmed and centered her. Refocused her. And today?

She had needed that. In order to do this thing being asked of her, Ruby needed to feel grounded in what was real.

And what was real was the solid wood of the wheel or drop spindle, and the feel of wool or silk between her fingers.

She stopped on the rapidly darkening northeast Portland street and looked at Sean's square, handsome face. Reflected twinkle lights danced across his skin.

"Do you believe in magic?" she asked him.

He shrugged his big shoulders. "I believe in people's ability to change the world by changing their minds. We cater to people's imaginations, don't we? That's how we make our bread and keep. And without imagination, nothing new would ever be built or made, and the change we say we want will never come to be."

Ruby huffed out a breath and pressed her hands against the rounded slope of her belly, trying to calm the strange butterflies jostling inside. She thought of Tempest's dark, startled eyes. The punk rock anarchist intensity of Daniel and Lawrence. She'd gotten so caught up in her business troubles lately, maybe she'd forgotten what that was like.

To remember that her actions had effect beyond her own life.

To feel as if, working with her punk-ass comrades, the world could change for the better.

Ruby just stood there, staring at her friend, then looked up to at the white flakes falling through the sky, dancing, as the streetlights switched on and the multicolored, twinkling bulbs shone. The lights spoke of the faith people had that shining lights in the darkest time of the year would lift their hearts. That maybe, just maybe, miracles could happen.

Wheel settled to her satisfaction, she closed the hatchback.

"Okay," she said to the gently falling snow, then straightened her neck and looked at Sean and then Carla. "Okay. You're right. Guess it's the season of taking risks because it's the only thing we can do."

"Welcome to adulthood, lass." A wry grin flickered across Sean's face and he opened his big arms. She stepped into the embrace. He held her close for a second before releasing her. It was just the comfort she needed. A little bit of big nerd courage, wrapped around her.

"Thanks, you two. I really appreciate it."

Carla gave her a quick hug. "No problem, Ruby. We like you, you know. Always happy to help. But it's freezing out here and we should really get going now. We need to see to our animals and get some dinner."

"See you at the park," Ruby said. "I'm going to run some errands and get food myself but should be there in a couple of hours."

"See you there," Sean replied. Carla was already unlocking their Prius and settling herself inside.

Ruby stood in the cold for another moment. Breathing in the cold air, she sent off a quick prayer to whoever it was that listened to such things.

"Keep us safe tonight," she said.

37

TEMPEST

Tempest stepped out of the cold dusk of late afternoon and into the bright warmth of Raquel's café, wiping her feet on the big mat laid out on the black and white checkerboard floor. Cassiel was behind the counter in a red apron, chatting with a customer, her tumbled russet curls shaking with laughter. It was good to see her laugh like that. A year ago she wouldn't have been.

The customer took his go cup of coffee and strode past Tempest, huge grin on his face.

"Hey there," Cassie said, still smiling. "Happy Solstice Eve."

"Hey there, yourself. Happy Solstice Eve. Can I get a green tea?" She perused the big chalkboard that hung between the counter and the tiny kitchen space. "And a spinach and turkey panini on GF bread?"

"Sure. Any cheese?"

"Swiss."

Up to that moment, Tempest hadn't been feeling too happy about Solstice Eve, but damn it, Cassie was right, just because some asshole decided to attack didn't mean he could ruin what had been a perfectly gorgeous winter day.

Tempest's thoughts believed that, anyway. And her body did, too. Her heart, though? That was a different story.

Her heart wanted to kick somebody's ass. Which was a change from the usual, at least. A Yule gift from Diana, maybe?

"Hey Tempest. Glad you could stop by." Raquel emerged from her office space, her curvy hips clad in her usual jeans, dreadlocks held back by a black headband. She wore a black T-shirt under the red "Raquel's" apron that was a match for Cassiel's and for the big red coffee mugs that were the café's signature.

"No prob. I didn't feel like cooking before tonight, anyway."

As Raquel made herself a latte, Tempest paid and took a small white teacup and the heavy metal teapot from Cassie. Raquel followed, steering her toward one of the booths along the side wall. Tempest set her tea down, flung her backpack onto a padded bench seat, and scooted in.

"So," Raquel said. "This sucks." She looked both worried and angry. Stern. A look Tempest bet shook Raquel's son, Zion, if he was ever on the receiving end of it.

"Something new happen? Or just the suck we've been dealing with?"

Raquel reached into her apron pocket and smacked a piece of metal on the table.

"Charlie found this. Under a D&D display."

"Oh, no." Tempest looked up at her mentor, heart racing, body not so happy with the beautiful day anymore.

The oily pewter of another Black Sun stared balefully at her from the tabletop.

"That's four now," Raquel said.

Tempest shook her head. "Five," she whispered.

Raquel's eyebrows shot up.

Tempest reached a hand toward the Black Sun, but did not touch it. "He planted one on my porch. We found it last night, and in the bustle of the meeting, forgot to text the people who weren't there."

"Well, damn. That's bad."

Tempest lifted the heavy bronze pot and poured the fragrant green tea into her small cup.

Raquel was still musing, hands wrapped around a big red coffee mug. Tempest could practically see her brain ticking over as she weighed the information.

"Five makes sense," she finally said. "For this kind of magic, he'll want some sort of movement. Not structure. He wants to disrupt structure."

"I don't get it," Tempest said, before blowing on the surface of her tea. "When we work with numbers, magically, three is the flowing structure, the building phase before the strict structure of four. Three has its own, natural structure, like the triangles found in nature. Four tends to be imposed from outside...."

Raquel shook her head, locks shaking heavily around her shoulders. "It's not a perfect theory, because there are exceptions to everything, but magically? It's just the way we tend to go, because it's a common thought form. You got that?"

Raquel became the teacher all of a sudden, her dark eyes holding steadily on Tempest's face, wanting to make sure she was taking in the lesson.

"It's like spells or prayers that get repeated over and over by a lot of people. They take on their own power?"

Raquel's face eased. "Yes. A self-powered spell has a different kind of power, but it requires more of the witch's will. If you can hook into a larger pattern and ride it, you don't need to pump as much of yourself into the spell."

"Okay. That makes sense."

Cassiel brought over Tempest's grilled sandwich. "Everything okay?"

"Not really," Raquel said, palming the Black Sun and slipping it back into her apron. "I just found out there's a fifth one of these suckers, and I don't like it."

"Shit," Cassie replied. The door opened, and a woman and two children walked in. "I gotta take this, but...damn. Tell me about it before tonight!" She turned and greeted the new customers, heading back toward the counter.

The smell of the grilled bread and cheese made Tempest's mouth water. Despite the tension in her stomach, she was hungry. She picked up her sandwich. The golden brown bread was hot.

Before she took a bite, she looked back at Raquel. "So, what about five?"

Raquel tapped a finger to her lips, eyes gazing at nothing that was in the room.

Tempest took a bite of sandwich. Delicious.

"Think of Tarot. Five," Raquel finally said, "is considered the number of chaos, or battle, or trying to build something on top of the old structure, or all of the above, depending on the context. It's the movement that takes us from the structure of four on through to the restoration of harmony in six."

Her eyes snapped back into focus. "At any rate, it was either going to be five or nine. But I'm hoping it's five."

"Why is that?"

Raquel leveled her gaze again. "Because that means we don't need to find any more of these fuckers before tonight."

38

RUBY

I t had been a weird day in the middle of a weird week, and it wasn't done yet. Tempest had texted Ruby for a ride to the action and a little surprised and pleased, Ruby had said yes.

It was full dark now, and freezing outside, and the soft snow continued to fall. Driving was a pain in the ass, and if Ruby didn't need to get all over town with a spinning wheel and a witch, there was no way she'd be on the roads. Luckily, traffic was light. People with more sense had stayed at home.

The car heater was cranked up and some old Rammstein blared from the car speakers. Ruby pulled the hatchback up Joshua's driveway toward the lit up space over the hulking garage. Tempest must have been watching for her, because before Ruby could even turn off the car, there she was, bundled up, locking her apartment door and stepping down the stairs, careful not to slip.

Through the snow, Ruby's headlights caught a flash of yellow hat and pale, almost ghostly cheeks.

The passenger door opened, letting in a blast of cold and an elfin creature swathed in black, and that cute as hell black and yellow scarf. Even if it was machine made out of crap materials. Maybe Ruby could weave her a special, custom version when she had the time.

Despite her tension, Ruby grinned.

"What's up?"

Tempest slung her backpack into the footwell and folded her tiny body into the hatchback's bucket seat before slamming the door.

And then those big dark eyes were blinking at her in the weird light cast by the reflection of Ruby's headlights bouncing off the garage door.

"Hi. Thanks for coming to get me."

Then the goldenrod and black hat was bent down, and gloved hands got busy tugging on the seatbelt and clicking the buckle into place.

Ruby hit a button and silenced the German metal.

Soon enough they were cruising down Hawthorne, headed for the bridge.

She could hear Tempest's soft breathing beneath the quiet rumble of the car and the noise of the street.

Ruby's hands were sweating on the wheel. She wiped first one, then the other, on her jeans, and turned down the heat.

As much as she loved having Tempest in her car, smelling her peppermint breath and the clean scent of laundry soap, there was no way to pretend this was some sort of weird date.

Ruby was feeling her nerves. Stomach clenching. Dinner sour on her tongue.

"You seem preoccupied. Is there anything else I should prepare myself for?" Ruby finally asked.

Tempest puffed out her cheeks and let out a noisy breath.

"We found a fifth amulet."

Ruby's heart leapt up into her throat and her head jerked toward Tempest, who was staring at her with those big, dark eyes, streetlights playing across her pale skin.

"That seems really bad, Tempest. What's this guy playing at?"

Turning her eyes back to the road, Ruby piloted her way toward the spot where Hawthorne turned into one way. She signaled and turned left on Twelfth, then left again on Madison. Ready to cross the bridge. Ready to face down whatever waited at the wedding cake of a mansion turned boutique hotel that stood on the waterfront, on the edges of downtown.

"Raquel thinks he's seeding chaos. Dissent. Just like we were talking about. The number five can mean that."

Ruby really was in some sort of demented game. Enchanted amulets, pixie guides, magic, and witches, and evil.

She cleared her throat.

"What else can it mean? The number five?" Traffic was light, thank goodness. The steel girders rose above them. It was almost time to turn off the bridge, look for parking. She hoped Sean and Carla were already there.

"It can mean diminishing life force. Shutting people out into the cold. Starvation."

Well, fuck.

"Where'd you find it?"

The light at the end of the off-ramp turned red. Ruby stopped behind an ancient Volvo festooned with peeling stickers.

"At Owlbear. Charlie's shop. He's Raquel's partner. I guess it was under a stand of pewter figurines."

"This really is some D&D shit," Ruby muttered.

"Yeah," Tempest agreed. "Except it's real."

TEMPEST

The sky was black with clouds and the air bit like a knife. The snow that had been falling just half an hour before had let up, leaving the lawns, sidewalks, and concrete balusters along the river walk covered in a light blanket of white.

Tempest stood, staring out at the river. The Willamette sparkled and the bridges were lit up as if they were on their way to a holiday party. The graceful white cables of Tillikum Crossing rose to the south of her, and the heavier steel and concrete of the Hawthorne and Morrison bridges spanned the river just north.

City of rivers. City of bridges. The place that she called home.

"It's weird, isn't it?" Lucy stood beside her, all wrapped up in a heavy work coat, black watch cap, and scarf. "Standing here, we're smack in the middle of so many other battles."

And she was right. Because of Tempest's chronic illness, she hadn't made most of the street actions the coven had tackled, but still, she'd been part of the magic. And she knew the taste of these places, from walking them before and after, and from the ætheric imprints the magic had made on her soul.

The ICE building was just south of the Tillikum bridge, and the coven—along with a large chunk of the city—had faced down fascists near the Morrison Bridge.

"Has the coven done the right things, do you think?" Tempest asked, staring out at the lights shimmering on the black river.

"What do you mean?" Lucy replied. Tempest could tell Lucy's eyes were on her, but she didn't turn her head. It was as if the water and the lights could answer the questions roiling inside of her.

"How do we know we're actually helping anything? How do we know our magic is aiming the right direction?"

Lucy gave a soft laugh. "We don't. We just do the best we can." Lucy gave her shoulder a squeeze. "I'm gonna go check in with the others. Don't be too long, okay?"

Tempest nodded, and returned to her vigil.

It had already been quite a day. She wasn't quite sure how she'd gotten through it. Last night's meeting had gone late, wiping her out. Everyone left en masse around eleven, including Ruby, who had snuck in a hug while Sean and Carla were getting their coats.

Tempest smiled at the thought. Whether it was Diana guiding her, or her magic increasing, she wasn't completely terrified of Ruby anymore. Oh, she still had nerves, but the car ride had been fine, and the thought of going on an actual date no longer made her want to hide.

But then she'd had two morning clients, and Moss and Lawrence wanted to coordinate, and she had stopped to check in with Raquel.

Finally, Raquel sent her home with orders for a nap.

Bless the Goddess's name. Her mentor was right, and now Tempest felt just revived enough to get through the night.

At least she hoped so. Chronic illness was a weird thing. But no matter what, she had to get through this Solstice Eve.

She looked up at the dark sky and saw the waxing crescent moon peeking out in a slender break between heavy clouds. A sign. Diana was with her.

Tempest drew the icy air deep into her lungs, raised her gloved hands, and began to pray.

"Thank you, Diana, for being with me this whole time. Thank you for whatever this new sense of courage is. Be with us tonight, and be with me always."

A peaceful sense of calm descended.

Tempest turned from the river, and walked toward the four-story Victorian whose wedding-cake façade was lit with hundreds of white twinkle lights. People with signs and banners gathered on the green lawn closest to the river, as other, well-dressed people, flowed toward the grand front doors on the harbor drive.

The party was starting.

As quickly as that thought entered her head, she saw Lucy and Alejandro, who'd clearly been watching for her. Ruby was just behind them.

Maybe once all of this was over, Tempest would finally get a first real date.

She hoped so. She really, really did.

40

RUBY

Ruby stood with Lucy and Alejandro between the fancy boutique hotel and the river, waiting for Tempest to come back from her meditation. Alejandro was nervous about leaving her alone, but Lucy insisted she had needed some time.

The messenger bag slung across her shoulder was filled with supplies. A water bottle. Her drop spindle. Some wool.

The big spinning wheel was still swaddled in the back of her car, in case they actually made it to Raquel's for the ritual the coven had originally planned. But "be prepared for anything," Moss had said, so drop spindle in her bag it was. Just in case.

Activists milled around the waterfront park in clusters, and it looked like the Sons of Ṣàngó—an African martial arts group—and ASP were conferring with some other groups. As always, Ruby was amazed at the organizational power of the Portland activist communities. Who knew they could get sixty people out on a cold winter's night, midweek? Especially around the holidays?

Moss loped up, practically vibrating with energy. "Folks

are almost ready to go. If I didn't love you all so much, I'd be in a bloc right now. Shit! I'm so ready to be up in this asshole's face!"

Alejandro bumped Moss's shoulder with his own. "Arrow and Crescent needs you for ritual. Sorry, man."

Ruby understood, though she was getting impatient with all of this waiting and watching, too. The whole two-pronged "if the energy feels right" action and ritual setup made her uneasy because she didn't fully understand it. But if the coven and other allied groups decided this was the way to go, who was she to argue?

And if Tempest needed time with the river to do whatever, Ruby was determined to be cool with that, too. She wanted to get to know Tempest, and this was part of the package.

Ruby could use some loyal and true in her life, and the witch seemed to have that in spades.

So, she stood between Alejandro and Lucy and watched, making sure Tempest was safe. That was one thing about direct actions. No matter how peaceful the plan was, no one should ever arrive or leave alone.

Too many things could happen.

"White nationalists run our city! The mayor and the Downtown Business Association are in bed with fascists!" A tall, thin, light-skinned Black man held a bullhorn mic to his mouth, the white bell of the bullhorn pointed toward the sky.

He led a group of folks in Black Bloc gear toward the front of the mansion-cum-hotel. Sons of Ṣàngó fanned out around their flank, adding another layer of protection.

"Here we go," Lucy said.

"What are we watching for?" Ruby replied.

"First of all, we want to let the media know that the

mayor is in deeper shit than they've dug up before," Lucy replied. "That's some material world action that will give our magic a boost. We try to work on as many levels as possible, you know?"

Ruby nodded, even though that only half made sense. She'd figure it out later.

Tempest rapidly approached them now, and Ruby let out a breath and rolled her neck. Wow, she was tense. The still air of the waterfront park suddenly roiled with the intensity that always came with actions.

"Second," Alejandro interjected, "we want to see how Brad and his father react. And as soon as Brad makes a move, so do we."

"That was all discussed last night during the meeting, but I'm still not clear what the point is."

"Because he likely planned his magic for later tonight, after the party was over, closer to the darkest time itself. As close to the moment of Solstice as he could get it," Alejandro said. He began to move toward the front of the lit-up white Victorian, whose massive, graceful porch was filled with partygoers. "At least, that's what I would do if I were him."

"And?" Ruby was still missing a key component.

"And if we flush him out here, spook him, we can direct the timing of the magic. We can force his hand," Lucy replied. "Get him to act sooner. And he'll want to. Riding people's anger will only increase his power. He'll want to take full advantage."

"At least, that's what we hope," Moss said, his face grim. "We're hoping to get back behind Raquel's wards to do the working, but if we don't make it? We're all here, right? And we can do magic wherever we are."

Tempest turned then, and trained those dark eyes on Ruby. They were steady now. It felt as if someone else was looking out from the deep brown that looked almost black in the weird mix of light and dark.

"I'm here because I want to see his face before Diana takes him down."

Tempest's usually soft voice was fierce. Sharp as a knife. Or the tip of a nocked arrow.

Ruby shivered, and wrapped her scarf more tightly around her neck.

"Then let's go see this asshole," she replied, and, tucking Tempest's arm inside her own, she strode across the grass toward the seething mass of light and sound.

41

TEMPEST

For once in her life, Tempest felt right.

She felt right, tucked close to Ruby.

She felt right, with the Goddess Diana hovering around her aura and knocking at the base of her skull.

She felt right, out here in the dark of winter, walking toward a group of angry activists and a bunch of wealthy people with their sleek hairdos and polished shoes, the rest of their finery tucked beneath expensive winter coats.

She barely felt the exhaustion skirting the edges of her mind.

She barely felt the cold.

What she felt was the magic of the night. The magic of a darkness so deep and long it could only be shattered by a winter sunrise, heralding the shortest day.

There was unnatural darkness, too, barely held at bay. She felt the pressure of it, building around her aura and the crowd.

Amazingly, Tempest didn't want to run away. She was exactly where she needed to be.

The noise of the crowd grew louder, penetrating the

cheap knit of her favorite yellow and black hat, beating against her ears.

Floodlights from the TV news lit up the front of the massive Victorian, obscuring the smaller holiday lights and the warm glow from inside the hotel.

Two of the Sons of Ṣàngó were drumming, and the deep bass sound reverberated against the big white building before rolling out into the night.

There were signs and banners up ahead, glowing in the lights, hand-lettered in black or stenciled in red.

There are Fascists in Our Government. One read.

Blood Money Funds Portland Coffers.

Ask the Mayor Who He's in Bed With.

"The signs look good. Lilith did a great job ferreting out this information," Ruby said.

Tempest agreed. Everyone had their talents. Everyone had a place.

Magic was for everyone who respected it, and maybe, someday, justice would be, too.

That was a thing she'd never thought before. She had lived with her own injustices and failings for so long. But maybe, just maybe, after all was said and done, the sun would rise on a world a little more magical and with a little more justice to go around.

But first, they had to turn the wheel.

She and Ruby and the others passed a phalanx of local newspaper and indie reporters, all with video cameras or big fuzzy microphones at the ready.

They didn't even notice her. That was good. She'd had years to practice not attracting notice.

Except his. *And Ruby's*, a little voice inside reminded her. Yeah. And Ruby's.

But for some reason, he had seen her, stalked her, tracked her down.

Deep in her bones, she knew he saw her as a weak link. A way into the coven. A broken window. An unlocked door.

She felt the healing seam from the crack in her aura's wards. It throbbed to the beat of the drums.

42

RUBY

She still wasn't sure how they were going to get out of this crush of energy and action and back to the sanctuary of Raquel's. Ruby didn't know much about real magic, but damned if she didn't know LARPing, or a well run D&D campaign.

There was no way the heroes left the main action to retreat to a safer place to attack. You stood your ground and worked from where you were.

But she wasn't a witch, was she? She didn't even play one in D&D. She was alternately a crafter or a basher, and that didn't change too much, whether in real life or gaming.

Mayor Patterson came out onto the porch, dressed in a camel-colored overcoat and a Burberry scarf. His dark hair gleamed under the news lights as if polished. His face was a study in "I'm a very serious man," though as they walked closer, Ruby could see a telltale twitch at the edge of his mouth that signaled he was pissed off.

And sure enough, just behind him, was Asshole Brad and his father. The other guy next to Martin Chadwick must have been Mr. Venture Capital whatever. At least, he had that look about him.

"What do you want to do?" She leaned close to Tempest so she didn't have to shout.

"I want him to look at me," Tempest replied, steering Ruby closer through the crowd. "And then I need to go. The crowd is too much."

It was relatively small, as Portland actions went, but Ruby could see that Tempest was sweating despite the cold, and her face looked even paler than usual.

"I got you. Your coven has you. And all these people?" Ruby looked at the intent and angry faces all around them. "They've got you, too."

And she knew that. She knew it as surely as she knew anything.

"Let's get you a little closer," Ruby said. "Get this done."

Tempest nodded, and Ruby helped her through the fray.

43

TEMPEST

The crush of bodies. The shouting. The lights. The feel of the longest night closing in around her. It was almost too much.

And in front of her, the vision of wealth was dazzling. Disturbing. The foster kid that still lived inside Tempest wanted to cut and run. Now. Her hands felt clammy inside her gloves, and her face was hot. She wanted to strip off her coat and hat and scarf, but knew that wouldn't help her. The heat came from within.

It was her power, shifting, growing. Her body hummed with it. Her bones ached with it, just like people who had sudden growth spurts talked about.

Diana? she thought. Layered images snapped into place. The waxing, crescent moon. The Black Sun. And an image of a Tempest-who-could-be, her aura shining, large and lustrous, around her small body.

She got the message. She needed to get bigger.

Remembering everything Brenda and Raquel had ever taught her, Tempest dug deep into the earth beneath her, and reached way up past the dark and clouds. She stood taller.

She felt Ruby's hand fall away.

"Give us some space!" Ruby's voice. Talking firmly to the people around her. "She needs some room."

Tempest breathed deeply, and drew up energy from the core of the earth. She exhaled power. She inhaled, and drew down the power of Diana's moon. She exhaled certainty.

She allowed her energy bodies to fill with the breath. To expand every time she breathed. Filling up with life and power. Filling with the promise of all she could become.

Yes.

She breathed and drew down and up and filled herself with the power of the earth in its constant, revolving dance around the mighty sun. She felt the Gods and Goddesses beloved of humans. She felt them dancing, too. And the stars and the trees and the cold night air.

Tempest grew large. As large as galaxies.

And then she opened her eyes.

Brad Chadwick stared down from the broad Victorian porch, eyes wide. Staring straight at her.

And he looked terrified.

From deep inside her, Tempest felt Diana laugh.

And so did she, the sound of her laughter blending with the sound of drums.

She reached her arms up, and flicked her fingers at his staring face. Felt him wince.

He turned his glossy blond head, and disappeared behind the mayor.

44

RUBY

The crowd had backed up, and several black clad bodies formed a shield around Ruby and Tempest. Something weird was happening to Tempest. She... Ruby couldn't explain it. She was still the tiny, waif-like girl, but, almost superimposed on top of that was one impressive, scary-as-hell woman.

Ruby was at a loss. All she knew was she needed to keep the witch safe.

"Ruby!"

She saw dreadlocks, and then Raquel's face appeared. Two anarchists let her in to the inner circle, quickly followed by Selene, Daniel, and Alejandro.

Their mingled scents of peppermint, coffee, tuberose, and amber made her head swirl.

"What's happening?" Raquel asked.

Ruby shook her head. "I'm not sure. I think she just cursed him. And she's...not quite like herself."

"Shit." Raquel turned to Daniel. "Moss and Lawrence. They're on our target?"

"Yes. They're keeping watch over the back door, along

with a couple of the Sons of Ṣàngó and a big heathen dude. Charlie's there, too. Joshua, Lawrence, and the rest of the coven are guarding the front."

"What do we do, now?" Ruby asked. "It doesn't seem like we should leave."

Raquel was staring at Tempest as if she wasn't really seeing her. Looked like some witchy thing.

"Tempest," she said gently. "You in there?"

Tempest's almost translucent eyelids fluttered, then she blinked, wincing at the lights, before closing her eyes again.

"Yeah. I'm here. But so is she."

"Who?" Ruby blurted.

"Diana."

Raquel turned to Daniel. "Okay. Plan B. We're doing ritual here. I want Cassie and the others to cast a sphere around this whole damn place. Contain that shit. Then we're going to proceed as close to the original plan as possible."

Daniel tapped some folks on the shoulder. The black-clad wall let him through.

Raquel looked around the small cluster centered around Tempest.

"Selene and Alejandro, you keep Tempest safe. I'll keep the connection going with the rest of the coven. They'll do what they do to keep things running with everyone else. Okay?"

Ruby stood there, shivering, worried about Tempest and a little pissed off. She'd let go of her common sense, taken a risk on this thing they called magic, and now they were freezing her out?

She planted her boots more firmly on the grass and, hands in her coat pockets, stuck out her chin.

"What about me?" That was aimed at Raquel.

"Oh, don't you worry, girl. You're on to do exactly what you signed up for."

Ruby blinked in confusion. She'd been so focused on Tempest...

Selene put a gentle hand on her shoulder. "You spin, Ruby. We need you to spin. The magic depends on it."

Ruby took in a huge breath of the cold night air and shook out her hands.

"Okay. Where should I set up?"

As soon as she spoke, the drums stopped, and so did the clamor all around. The sudden stillness rocked the waterfront park. The only sounds were some cars driving by and confused voices from the Victorian's veranda.

Then, into the winter's night, a woman's voice began to speak, finding its own rhythm. "By earth. By flame. By wind. By sea."

It was Cassiel. At least, Ruby thought so. Then other voices joined in. "By moon. By sun. By dusk. By dark. By witch's mark."

A lone drum joined in, punctuating the voices. The air began to feel strange. Thicker. More tangible.

Ruby didn't see how that was possible.

Raquel, Alejandro, and Selene joined in. Tempest, eyelids fluttering, mouthed the words.

"We consecrate this holy ground, with sight and sound, and breath twined 'round. With will and love, from below to above..."

The pressure was building. Ruby could feel it, pressing against her.

"Let the magic portals open!" The weird poem ended with a shout.

And the big news station lights popped, plunging the park into darkness.

45

TEMPEST

The painful lights were gone. Tempest blinked. It was dark, but only for a moment. As her eyes adjusted, she saw the golden glow of the Victorian's porch lights come on, and the white twinkle lights traced the balustrades again.

She squeezed Alejandro's hand, then Selene's. But there was someone else...

Ruby. She sought out those red lips and matching hat. The hair as black as night. The curvy body encased in layers against the cold. That face, with its smooth golden skin, and rounded cheeks, so different from Tempest's own. Gorgeous.

But she looked tense. Troubled.

The Goddess within Tempest smiled to see it, and Tempest did, too. It meant that Ruby cared.

"You're still here," she said. "You didn't run away."

Ruby swallowed and shook her head. "I didn't run away."

"I'll be fine. Okay? Just turn the wheel." She placed a gloved hand on Ruby's cheek and looked into her eyes. "We need you to turn the wheel."

Ruby nodded. "I understand."

Tempest nodded back, then dropped her hand. She wasn't certain if Diana had just spoken, or her, or both. Maybe it didn't matter. She had touched Ruby's cheek and looked into her eyes.

And that was something.

Then, with a huge breath, Tempest called up earth and called down sky again. She drew down the power of the waxing crescent moon, and felt Diana shift restlessly inside her.

"Diana, you of the crescent, and the arrow in swift flight, you of the hunt, I honor you. I entreat you. I ask for your aid. Send your hounds forth. Track this evil in our midst."

Maybe Tempest was becoming a priestess. After all this time.

46

———

RUBY

Ruby was having trouble concentrating. She knew she was supposed to be doing something but despite the crowd around their little cleared space, she was freezing, and things in the park were getting freaky. Mainly, *Tempest* was getting a little freaky.

The voice coming out of Tempest's slender throat had changed, becoming hollow, almost keening. It sounded like wind scraping bare branches against rooftops. It sounded like night and darkness and cold.

"You have my will. You have my aid. You have my promise. This thing you ask of me shall be done."

Tempest didn't sound like that at all. *It wasn't fucking Tempest.*

As Ruby watched, Tempest's hands shook, rising from her thighs. Her gloved fingers jerked and danced in the air, as if she held a rattle in each hand.

Selene's white face leaned close to Ruby's. Her black-painted lips moved, voice carrying the short distance to Ruby's ears, barely cutting through the weirdness of whatever was talking through Tempest.

"Please. Spin," Selene said. "Sean is bringing a stool in for you, but if you can, we need you to start right away. Shit's already going down."

That much was clear.

Ruby grabbed her water bottle from the messenger bag and took a swallow to wet her dry throat and mouth. Then she re-capped it, and drew out her favorite dark walnut spindle.

They needed her to turn the wheel? The drop spindle in her bag would do.

She switched to fingerless gloves, split open a gallon bag of wool, drew out a piece of leader yarn, and wound it around the long center shaft.

All tools weren't the same, but that didn't mean she couldn't work with what she had. Ignoring Tempest for the moment, she concentrated on threading the leader through the hook at the top of the flat disc of the whorl. Then she split off some wool from the hank in her bag, and with careful fingers, joined it with the leader. Fiber to fiber. Thread to thread.

And so it began, simply. Making yarn the way yarn had been made for centuries.

Basic human activity. Continuing the cycles of creation.

As she spun, snow began to fall again in lazy flakes. It was going to be a challenging spin.

She hoped she was up for it, exposed fingertips and all.

47

TEMPEST

Wet, cold flakes of snow kissed her cheeks. Tilting her head back, Tempest stuck out her tongue, catching the cold in her mouth. It tasted of change.

She felt the coven around her, gathered like bright flames, there on the edges of the mighty Willamette. They breathed as if they were one organism. They breathed fire and incense. They breathed river water and loam. They breathed with the darkness. They breathed cold and warmth, isolation and companionship. They breathed anger and hope.

They breathed life, and they breathed death.

And she breathed, too. She breathed as Tempest. As a witch on the cusp of a life she could barely understand. And she breathed as Diana, healer, protector, and hunter.

And tonight, the hunt was on the prowl.

She felt the astral hounds release. Felt the bunching of their muscles and the saliva dripping from their jaws. She felt the icy wind on their long, slim snouts, and snow beneath their graceful paws.

Raquel pressed something into Tempest's hand. It was

small. Thin. Ridged. It felt oily beneath her fingertips. It felt like death. As if someone had taken the sunwise wheel and was slowly, painfully, turning it backwards. Against the moon. Against the tides. Against the cycles all the creatures of the earth needed to survive.

"Time flows backward," spoke the Goddess. "Against the cycle. And he is one who seeks to pervert and disrupt time."

She felt a stirring in the coven. Heard their whispers. She felt the crowd around her roar. She clacked her jaws and tasted the blood of the hunt.

Picking up her bow, she aimed into the darkness, unwavering. Seeking through the twinkling lights and snow.

Seeking out the slender knife blade of the crescent.

She would aim. And would aim true.

48

RUBY

Things got stranger. Tempest was growling out a string of brittle, keening words. Ruby's stomach lurched. She thought she might be sick.

Just then, Sean and Carla came, easing their way past the guardians that were the Black Bloc. Sean had a small stool and Carla carried blankets.

Alejandro waved them over and leaned into Ruby.

"Keep breathing," he said.

"Here you go, lass," Sean said, setting the stool onto the snow-covered lawn. He gently pushing her down. As soon as she was seated, Carla tucked a light, warm blanket around her shoulders.

"Thank you." Ruby looked up at two people whom just recently she would have named as con and fair acquaintances, but who she now saw were rapidly becoming friends.

They both shrugged at her.

"It's the least we could do," Carla said, while Sean scanned the crowd, his face tense. He crossed his arms over his massive chest and stepped to one side of Ruby. Carla did the same.

Just as Tempest had Alejandro and Selene, now Ruby had her own personal guardians. It was weird, but she was glad for it all the same.

Alejandro turned back to her and frowned.

"Are you ready?"

She nodded.

"Good. No matter what happens, just spin, okay? That's why you're here tonight. Just focus on that. Sean and Carla have your back."

"Okay."

Ruby took a breath of the icy air and pinched a section of wool, drawing out a short segment. Then she flicked the spindle, and began again.

"Thank Goddess," Alejandro muttered, then turned back to Tempest, who was keening wildly now.

Ruby caught the hint of desperation in Alejandro's voice. As if he really needed her to do this thing but didn't want to panic her. The way a parent talked to a child when danger was near and they needed to keep that child safe.

Ruby blocked out what was happening around her, and focused on the motion of her fingers, the feel of the wool, and the weight of the spindle.

The spindle dropped and turned, she drew the wool out into a strong, smooth thread, and wound it around the spindle, before starting the process again, with a clockwise flick of her hand. The rhythm was continuous, her whole body in the flow. She felt Carla's hand on her back, a small weight through the layers of clothing. Connection.

"Turn the wheel, hermana. Turn the wheel!" Alejandro said, as if, though he no longer looked her way, he was connected to her somehow. Focused on Tempest, surrounded by a shouting crowd, aware of Ruby with some witch's sense.

And somehow, in the moment, Ruby felt all of that, too.

And so there, sitting on a low stool in falling snow, surrounded by a crowd, with the woman she was rapidly falling for taken over by some Goddess...

There in the cold night, Ruby did what she knew best.

She created something. She focused on the turning wheel, and spun.

49

TEMPEST

Witch and Goddess, Goddess and witch. The world spun within and around her. She felt the strength of the coven. She felt the turning of the tide.

She felt herself, marked by two opposing magics, but instead of feeling at war within herself, Tempest felt her power.

She felt the sun, straining against the darkness. She felt a wheel, spinning something new. Spinning threads of warmth, and of connection. She felt the coven catch those threads. They would weave them with their magic.

The people would feed the magic with their strength. Their power.

But the amulets were strong. The one she held felt like poison in the witch's hand. It was a sun like no other. A harbinger of the end. When the world would crack and cold would reign. When warmth would not return as it should, to balance the chill darkness.

"A world out of balance is a world bent on destruction. A world in chaos fights itself. And dies."

Goddess. Tempest's consciousness fought to hold on.

Fought to remain grounded in what was real. Her body shook and trembled with the strain. It was too much. She was too ill. Too unprepared. Not talented enough. Not good enough. Not...

"Tempest! Stop it! Come back!" Raquel's voice was a slap against her face. Tempest rocked backward, held by warm, strong arms. Alejandro. And Selene.

"Let the Goddess do her work." That was Selene's voice in her ear. Calm. Cool. But worried. "Open to her. You can do this."

"We've got you," Raquel said. "Never forget that. You matter to us, and we've always got your back."

"Always, hermana, always," Alejandro said.

Always.

Unless time was at an end.

50

RUBY

Rocking on the stool, booted feet planted in the snow, Ruby spun wool as if her life depended on it. Beneath her layers, her T-shirt was soaked through. Her toes gripped the insides of her boots, rapidly freezing despite thick wool socks.

"Turn the wheel, Ruby," Carla said. "Turn the wheel."

And so she did.

51

TEMPEST

Tempest's consciousness flew with Diana's arrow. She shot up into the night, the swirling snow and lights. High above the city, she flew. Straight. True. Aiming for the moon.

52

RUBY

R uby caught movement from the corner of her eye. It was Moss. Moving toward her.

He crouched next to Ruby and stared into the wheel. For a long while, he simply held position, like he was a snake, charmed by a holy man's flute.

"It's holding," he finally said. Then he blinked and said. "Is there a way to pass me some of that yarn?"

"Not unless I stop spinning. And since I don't want Alejandro there to bite my head off, that's not going to happen."

Intensity rolled off of Moss in waves, but Ruby remained calm. Focused. Her hands kept at their work, as if they had minds of their own.

The spindle turned.

"Carla," Moss said, "I'm going to take your hand. You stay attached to Ruby. We're going to feed the magic out into the crowd. Okay?"

Carla said something to Moss. Ruby kept pinching, winding, and pulling.

"Just keep going, Ruby! We're passing the thread magically."

Ruby didn't reply. The witches could do whatever the hell they needed to. She just needed to spin.

Then she swore the air around her changed.

Whatever Carla, Moss, and the witches were doing, it was working. She felt the thread of life, spinning outward. She felt Carla and Moss, grabbing hold. It was the weirdest sensation. Her fingers stuttered on the yarn for a moment. She breathed in and steadied them.

Hand to hand, the connection passed into the snow and dark, fed by the spinning, turning dynamo that she just couldn't stop.

And Ruby felt the truth of that, somewhere in her bones. The thread she spun connected everything.

She didn't know how. And she didn't know why. But there it was.

And her job was to sit in the falling snow with a bunch of witches. With Black and Asian activists and white anarchists—with the Satanists, atheists, radical Christians, Buddhists, and Jews who always showed up when shit went down...

Her job was to spin as if her life depended on it.

As if life itself depended on it.

53

TEMPEST

She saw it then. And felt it. The pattern. It was not a five-pointed star. No upside-down pentagram greeted her. No.

It was a spear. An arrow. Shot straight down from the hotel near the conference center, it raced toward the Inner Eye, toward Tempest's apartment, and on down to Foster, to Charlie's.

He had let them think it would be a pentagram, but that was just a feint, to throw her hounds off the scent. The bad magician had used the building chaos and disruption of the number five and harnessed it with his bare will.

He had fashioned an energetic spear to crack Portland in two. Not east to west or north to south. He cut through them all. A diagonal slash. Northwest to southeast.

And this mansion on the waterfront was not in line with his pattern.

Perhaps the witches could use this. Boost their magic.

"I have you now," Diana said. The voice fell like stones, tumbling from Tempest's mouth.

The witch straightened her spine. The Goddess called her hounds.

"Form the amulets in one straight line!" Tempest shouted.

She felt the witches scramble to comply.

Somewhere, a wheel whirled, spinning out a skein of day and night. A low chanting arose from around her.

"We spin with the earth in the darkness. We spin around the sun.

We spin with the earth in the dark night sky. We spin and day is won."

The words shifted and changed, morphing in the space around witch and Goddess.

"Light and dark dance day and night. Life and death kiss in the cold.

The pregnant night gives birth to dawn, the new born from the old."

And the amulets were in a line. She felt them. Saw the cunning, evil pattern that built—Black Sun to Black Sun. The Great Undoing. She felt it in her bones.

54

RUBY

"Get me more wool!" Ruby was running out, but didn't want to break cadence to reach for more.

"Where is it?" That was Carla's voice.

"My bag."

"Moss, you take my place!" Carla said. There was a brief delay as Moss's hand replaced Carla's on her back. Ruby tried to remain calm, to focus on the wool and yarn. But she didn't want to find out what would happen if she came to the end of the unspun wool.

She heard rustling, and then a soft cloud of wool was there, pressing against the back of her hands.

"Feed it to me, one tuft at a time. Okay? I can't stop."

"How much?" Carla asked.

"Doesn't matter. Just do it."

She was one with the spindle and the wool. She was one with the motion of the whorl and her fingers. One with the rocking cadence of spinning one thing into another.

And—hand to hand to hand—the witches and anarchists fed the magic outward. Yes. She called it magic. She felt the spark of it, as palpable as the wool between her fingers. It formed a flowing skein, moving out into the crowd. Into the longest night. Forming circles within circles within circles.

They spooled her magic outward, attempting to weave the magic into a pattern. A pattern Ruby somehow knew, though she had never spun or woven it before.

55

TEMPEST

er bones vibrated inside of her. The pattern was set. Another pattern opposed it.

But was an arrogant man a match for a Goddess and a witch?

Witches and anarchists wove day into night, flow into chaos. Pattern met pattern. Life met death. Rising met falling. New met old.

The cunning, slender hounds were back, dark eyes rolling, mouths tinged with spit and red. She tasted him. His magic. His blood. He was wounded. Angry. She felt that in her breath and in her bones.

The virgin Goddess would take her due. She was complete, sovereign unto herself. His blood on the jowls of the hounds would serve as a reminder that he was not, and would never be, whole.

The power built. The Goddess cracked the witch's mind. Diana was free, howling in the night, baying with her hounds, teeth gleaming in the darkness, eyelids peeled back, laughing in the snowy winter air.

And, with a mighty crash, high above the city of Portland, arrow met spear. A clash. A crack. A sonic boom.

The witch's body fell, crashed into the snow.

Scattering a line of amulets in her wake.

56

RUBY

Ruby heard shocked voices and her head jerked up. She saw Tempest go down.

"Keep spinning," Moss shouted in her ear. He had to shout. The crowd in the park and on the mansion porch had grown unbearably loud.

Shouting. Fast talking. Moaning. Was that Tempest's voice? And the weird chanting that grew louder and louder.

"Light and dark dance day and night. Life and death kiss in the cold.

The pregnant night gives birth to dawn, the new born from the old."

Whatever that meant.

"Ruby!"

The urgency in Moss's voice was real. Ruby realized her fingers were still.

"Shit!" Quickly, she fed in more wool. Her fingers flicked the whorl. The spindle dropped and spun again.

"Take the amulets!" Raquel's voice rose over the clamor. "Throw them in the river!"

Boots scrabbling, shoving, pushing. Chanting rising, and

then movement. The space inside the tight, cleared circle was calm.

Ruby breathed deeply, icy air spiking her lungs.

Her hands never stopped their work. Spinning wool into the yarn she wound securely on her spindle. Feeling the weird magic of the night as it passed through the crowd from hand to hand.

Carla handed her another tuft of wool. The witches continued their work. So did Ruby.

She just hoped Tempest was okay.

57

TEMPEST

Tempest came to, shivering and moaning. Her back ached. The ground was hard and cold. Damp seeped through her jeans.

The inside of her right wrist burned as if branded. She remembered the vision she'd had before blacking out. Diana had marked her with a crescent moon, searing the shape into her flesh. She had two marks now. The tiny tattooed pentagram on her left wrist, and the crescent on the right.

Her life was one with the Goddess's now. Pentacle and crescent moon, she was a witch always and forever, no matter what.

In the vision, Diana had told Tempest that her insides were slowly repairing themselves, so her immune system should stop going on offense all the time, but she would need to be careful for the rest of her life. If that was true, it felt like a decent compromise.

But for now, it was enough that she was alive, and back in her body. At some point soon, she'd probably be grateful for that, but in the moment, she just hurt.

Someone threw a soft blanket over her, and gently lifted her, tucking another beneath her. She helped as best she could, then burrowed in like a small, wounded animal, seeking shelter from the cold and the terrors of the night.

Except she had been one of the terrors, hadn't she? She blinked, aware of the warm bodies of her coven mates around her.

She was Tempest now, but she had also been Diana, hunting someone down.

Not someone. *Him.* Brad.

Tempest's eyes snapped wide and, heart racing, she pushed at the blanket, struggling to rise.

"The amulets!"

"Shhh," Raquel said. "Can't you feel it? You broke the pattern. Moss and Lucy ran the amulets to the river. They should be sinking to the silt now. Washed clean."

Tempest felt it then. The winding, twining, counter-sunwise energy was gone. In its place was warm breath, human bodies moving around her, and the cleansing, snowy cold of night.

"You did it. I have no idea how, girl, but you did it," Raquel said.

"Diana. It was all her. Diana and her hounds."

"Bless the arrow and the crescent," she heard Brenda murmur. Her mentor's soft hands tugged Tempest's hat down firmly over her ears.

If Brenda and Raquel were here and calm, that meant it was going to be okay.

Tempest lay back down, this time with her head cradled in Raquel's generous, comforting lap. The buzzing energy that had filled her was gone. She was depleted.

She couldn't hold on to consciousness anymore.

"Too tired," she murmured, and felt Raquel's hands

stroke her head. Another thought half-surfaced through the fog that had settled in her brain. She tensed again, eyes fluttering.

"Ruby?"

"Ruby's fine." Alejandro's face hovered over her. A hint of whiskey and cologne. "She's with Moss and Selene, but I'll go check on her for you, too. She did great."

Tempest felt him move away. She relaxed, no longer able to resist the pull of darkness.

"We'll need to carry her out of here,." she heard Raquel say.

And then, snow falling gently on her face, she slept.

58

RUBY

Selene laid a hand on Ruby's arm.

"You can stop now. Thank you. You...you did great. You were damn amazing, actually."

Her fingers ached, her back was stiff, her feet were blocks of ice, and her butt was going numb. She stretched her back and massaged her hands before shaking them out.

In the twinkle lights and darkness, the snow fell on, coating the trees that reached toward sky and the eaves of the mansion. It was beautiful.

"All right, lass?" Sean loomed above her, holding out a huge, mittened hand.

"I think so. I'm more worried about Tempest. Is she...?"

Ruby allowed herself to be pulled upright and stomped her boots, wincing at the tingling needles in her toes. She looked past Sean's bulk toward where she had seen Tempest fall. Carla tucked the blanket more firmly around her shoulders.

"Thanks."

Tempest was bundled up in blankets of her own, passed out on Raquel's lap like some Pagan pieta. In the weird, wavering mix of holiday lights, Ruby could see purple shadows beneath her closed eyes.

Alejandro caught her eye, nodded, and walked over.

"Will she be okay?" Ruby asked when he got close.

"She should be fine." But his voice sounded worried. "We need someone to carry her out, though. Sean?"

"On it."

Ruby went to follow, but Carla stopped her. "Let them take care of it. You can see her later. Let me help you pack up your stuff, okay?"

"She's sleeping anyway," Alejandro said. "But she asked about you right before she passed out again."

Ruby nodded, mouth pinched in worry, gazing after Sean. She watched him pick Tempest up, so gently. Watched Raquel and Brenda tuck the blankets around her. They all trudged off in the snow, avoiding the remaining crowd.

Ruby knew there was no way she could help Tempest. Not now. But she wished there was.

Then she remembered. Nazi boy.

"Brad?" she asked Selene. "What happened there?"

"He's gone," Selene replied. "Daniel and Lawrence caught up to him out at the back of the mansion. Must've gone out a rear entrance."

The pale Goth witch grimaced. "He was definitely doing magic. He had a Black Sun the size of his hand, apparently, but as soon as he saw them, he dropped it and ran. A bunch of folks chased him to his car."

Ruby flexed her fingers against the cold.

"Daniel picked up the big medallion," Alejandro chimed in. "He, Lawrence, Moss, and Lucy are dealing with it."

Ruby exhaled, then wrapped the end of the yarn around the metal hook, severing it from the tuft in her hand. Then she looked out at ragtag group of activists who stood on the snowy lawn. Most of them had dropped hands, but she could almost see ghost images of the spiraling pattern they had formed just moments ago.

"Hey!" Two black-clad people loped up, hoodies up, scarves over their faces. "Can we have some of that yarn?"

"What?" Ruby asked.

"For bracelets," the second person said. "Moss said you were spinning magic yarn."

Ruby grinned. It was nice to smile. "Sure. Of course."

She drew a pair of silver scissors from her bag, clipped off two lengths from the end of the fat cone of yarn wound around the spindle, and dropped them into gloved hands.

"If anyone else wants yarn, just send them by."

"Solid. Thanks!"

When she looked back at Selene, the witch's dark lipsticked lips were curved into a small smile.

"Everyone got a little magic tonight, didn't they? That's good."

Ruby nodded. Everyone got a little magic. Including her.

And then, people were moving again. Heading toward the broad porch of the Victorian mansion.

"*White supremacists out of business! Mayor! Out! Now!*" The crowd shouted. The news cameras filmed.

But the porch was empty. All the wealthy Portlanders had gone inside to the warmth, to drink champagne and eat canapés.

She hoped they were ashamed of themselves.

And she hoped some indie journalist had enough leads now to dig up the whole story. To bring the assholes down.

And get rid of the corrupt mayor once and for all.

59

TEMPEST

S he was being carried by a solid, moving mountain. And she had left the spinner behind.

She didn't want to leave the spinner behind. The weaver. The red-lipped woman with the lush body and ready smile.

"Ruby?" she asked, eyes still closed tight.

"Shhh, lass. Ruby's fine. She'll see you soon, okay?"

Tempest's eyes closed again. She let herself be carried through the cold and snow. She was safe for now.

They were all safe.

Except one man, still out there. Chased across the astral planes by Diana's hounds. She could feel them out there, running, but Tempest was too tired to call them back. She wasn't sure she even had the power.

Once a Goddess got something in her teeth, sometimes it was hard to let it go.

But witches? They were human. She would have to trust Diana to do what the Goddess deemed fit.

60
____

RUBY

It had been a weird couple of weeks, but it was done now. Or at least, she'd thought so.

But knocking on the door of the Southeast Portland Craftsman, and being welcomed in by an excitable teen who had introduced himself as Zion before racing off into the kitchen, Ruby felt in her bones just how weird things still were.

She stood in striped wool socks, having shucked her coat and boots, in a warm living room with a red sofa that matched her sweater, and crackling fire, surrounded by witches. But the witches, the fire, the art on the walls all faded to the background.

All she could see was one pale face, wearing blue today, turned toward her, ensconced on that red sofa. It was as if the whole room had hushed. As if there wasn't a family party happening here, where she was a relative stranger. As if the bottle of wine wasn't still in her hands. As if the tall, broad man named Charlie but who looked like Thor wasn't still standing right beside her, re-introducing Ruby to the people she'd shared the most bizarre night of her life with.

All Ruby saw was Tempest, with those doe-dark eyes and pale pink lips.

"Hey," Ruby said. Then she was crouched at the back of the couch, that pale, luminous face a scant foot from her own. "Are you okay? Last time I saw you…"

"I was passed out in the snow?"

"Yeah. That. And you didn't really answer my texts." Ruby gave a wry grin and was vaguely aware of Charlie taking the wine bottle from her hands. Hands free, she slid her right hand up to the back of the couch, hoping…and Tempest slid one her tiny hands into Ruby's palm.

"Sorry about that. I was wiped out. I stayed in bed for a couple days, which made my cat happy, but yeah, I'm better now. A lot better. Thanks for coming. And thanks for checking in on me."

Ruby let out a sigh of relief. She'd been damn worried, especially when her texts didn't get much more of a reply than *I'm just tired. Hanging low for a few. Can we get together when I'm feeling better?*

And then the text came inviting her for Christmas at Raquel's. *If you're not busy,* it said. *I'd love to see you.*

"Why don't you have a seat, Ruby?" Raquel said from across the room. She was poking at the fire. "There's still some time before dinner."

Ruby squeezed Tempest's hand, then skirted the sofa and scanned the room. Aw, shucks. The only spot was in the center of the couch, next to curled-up Adorable Witch who still looked so vulnerable, but who Ruby now knew was really, fucking brave.

Ruby raised an eyebrow her way. Tempest nodded, so Ruby plopped her black jean–covered ass down. A mug of tea was pressed into her hands. It was warm and smelled of cloves and ginger.

Their knees pressed together on the couch, and when Ruby looked, Tempest was smiling.

"So," Alejandro said, clearing his throat. "I suppose you want to know what exactly happened the other night."

She didn't one hundred percent know if she wanted that knowledge. But shit had definitely gone down, so....

"Mainly, I want to know what happened to Tempest, here." She patted Tempest's knee and left her hand there. Tempest didn't move away.

Raquel laughed. "I'll try to explain, but this is going to take more time than we have today." She leaned forward in her chair, piercing her with her eyes. "But I want you to know, all of us are here for you. If you ever need more explanation, or need us to stop talking about it, or need any help whatsoever, we're here."

"You did the coven a boon," Lucy chimed in. "You're part of the family now. Just like Daniel and Lawrence, who you should probably talk to about all of this, by the way."

Heart fluttering and mind racing, Ruby drank some of the spiced tea, trying to buy time.

What did she have to lose?

"Okay. Hit me with it."

Tempest grabbed Ruby's free hand and held it. It felt good.

"We needed the power of the wheel," Tempest said. Her voice, which had been so harsh and discordant the night of the action, was soft now. But still strong. Steady. "He was trying to turn back the power of the sun. We needed someone who could keep the wheel turning the right way, no matter what happened to any of us. You did that."

Ruby looked at her, but didn't quite know what to say. She had felt what happened. Even called it magic. But that didn't mean she understood. Not really.

"There's a thing called sympathetic magic," Raquel said. "Your spinning provided that, giving the coven a base to work from. As Tempest and the Goddess took on the Black Sun, you helped bolster the power of our sun, which was waiting to be reborn on Solstice."

"Like Jesus?"

The witches laughed.

"Well, more like Mithras or Ra," Lucy said, "but yeah, Jesus will do."

61

TEMPEST

Finally, enough of the story came out that Ruby seemed satisfied. For now. Tempest could tell she was still worried about her though, which felt kind of nice.

"Yesterday, Daniel got a call. Turns out our boy Brad spent Solstice in the hospital," Alejandro said. "Lawrence called me, and Moss did some more digging. Brad was driving in the snow after being chased off. Too fast. He swerved to avoid a dog, hit some ice, and smacked into a wall. He'll be fine, looks like, but I think he'll be out of commission for a while."

A dog. *Holy, Diana. The hounds.*

"And his dad?" Ruby asked. "Wasn't he the real problem?"

Alejandro gave an almost feral grin. "Daddy is facing embezzlement charges. Turns out the Downtown Business Association isn't very happy with him right now. And the mayor is in deep shit. Seema Gupta, an indie journalist, has been keeping me updated. It's a pretty big story for her, so she's thrilled."

Which meant Tempest and the coven were safe, at least

for now. And Tempest had a gorgeous woman who actually seemed to want to be sitting next to her. And it had taken a few days, but she really was starting to feel better, just like Diana had said.

Tempest ran her fingers over the soft, naked skin where the crescent had been branded into her astral form. Maybe she should get the mark tattooed, as a reminder of what existed on the ætheric planes.

It seemed like Diana had a lot more to teach her, about healing, and bravery, and a lot of other things. The crescent was a reminder of that.

And a reminder that she was going to need the coven's help, no matter how strong she became.

Alejandro and Selene had been trying to gently pound it into her head that she wasn't alone anymore. Sitting here, in Raquel's cozy space, surrounded by people she loved, Tempest felt that.

She belonged.

She had the coven and maybe even her first girlfriend, if things worked out.

Ruby. With her dark eyes and golden skin. With her badass, confident walk, and those red, red lips. The woman whose strong, lush body was gently pressed against Tempest's.

"Who wants to help me in the kitchen?" Raquel asked. "Zion's been in there making biscuits and it smells like they're just about done, which means we should get the rest of the food out."

Sure enough, the smell of hot biscuits had joined the mingled scents of the hearth fire and spicy tea.

"Not you, Tempest," Raquel said as she walked past. "You either, Ruby. This one time, you're a guest."

One by one, the coveners who could attend, and their

partners, rose and offered help. With a clattering of teacups and some laughter, they headed through the swinging kitchen door.

For this first time since the night the amulet was found on her stairway, she and Ruby were alone.

Be brave, Tempest. She inhaled deeply and realized that the magic had changed her. She was still shy, sure, but she didn't feel terrified anymore.

She sent up a quick prayer to thank Diana, then smiled and turned her head to find Ruby staring at her.

Waiting.

Heart pounding in her chest, Tempest *leaned*. Just a little bit. Testing. Asking. Offering.

Ruby's eyes brightened, and she leaned right back. Their lips met. Soft. Warm. Ruby tasted like cinnamon and cloves. She tasted of hope, and laughter, and the promise— someday—of sex.

The kiss deepened, and their lips parted. They tasted one another. Ruby made a small sound in her throat, then pulled away, coming up for air.

"Oh girl, you have no idea how good you taste. How long do you think they'll be busy in the kitchen?"

Tempest laughed. "If I taste as good as you do, I think I know. And they'll be back soon, sounds like."

The noises in the kitchen definitely sounded as if plates were being stacked, and the scent of ham fresh out of the oven was a high note above the smell of the crackling fire.

Ruby rested her forehead against Tempest's.

"My housemates are out of town. After we hang out here for a while, would you want to go back to my place?" she said. "We can take it slow, but I'd like to spend more time with you."

It felt so intimate, to sit forehead to forehead with this woman.

It felt a little bit dangerous, but still safe.

Right.

Her right wrist tingled with that astral crescent moon.

"If you're sure we can still take it slow, then yes," Tempest replied. "I'd like that. Very much."

Ruby kissed her once again. The noises from the kitchen increased.

"Merry Christmas, Tempest," she said.

"Happy Yule," Tempest replied.

And it was. It really, really was.

REVIEWS

*Reviews can make or break a book's success.
If you enjoyed this book, please consider telling a friend, or
leaving a short review at your favorite booksellers or on
GoodReads.
Many thanks!*

*Visit thorncoyle.com for a free short story collection and to
sign up for a monthly newsletter.*

ACKNOWLEDGMENTS

I give thanks to the cafés of my new hometown, Portland, Oregon. All you baristas are fine human beings.

Thanks also to Leslie Claire Walker, my intrepid first reader, to Dayle Dermatis, editor extraordinaire, and to Lou Harper for my covers. Gratitude to Jacki and Lyssa for expert consultation (any liberties taken are my own) and to my writing buddies for getting me out of the house.

Speaking of house...thanks as always to Robert and Jonathan.

Big, grateful shout out to the members of the Sorcery Collective for spreading the word and to Jack and Myke for extra typo catching.

And last...

Thanks to all the activists and witches working your magic in the world. This series is for you.

ALSO BY T. THORN COYLE

Fiction Series

The Panther Chronicles (Complete)

To Raise a Clenched Fist to the Sky

To Wrest Our Bodies From the Fire

To Drown This Fury in the Sea

To Stand With Power on This Ground

The Witches of Portland (complete)

By Earth

By Flame

By Wind

By Sea

By Moon

By Sun

By Dusk

By Dark

By Witch's Mark

The Steel Clan Saga (2020/2021)

We Seek No Kings

We Heed No Laws

We Ride at Night

Non-Fiction

Evolutionary Witchcraft

Kissing the Limitless

Make Magic of Your Life

Sigil Magic for Writers, Artists & Other Creatives

Crafting a Daily Practice

ABOUT THE AUTHOR

T. Thorn Coyle has been arrested at least four times. Buy them a cup of tea or a good whisky and they'll tell you about it.

Author of the *The Witches of Portland*, the alt-history urban fantasy series *The Panther Chronicles*, the novel *Like Water*, and two story collections, her multiple non-fiction books include *Sigil Magic for Writers, Artists & Other Creatives*, and *Evolutionary Witchcraft*.

Thorn's work appears in many anthologies, magazines, and collections. They have taught magical practice in nine countries, on four continents, and in twenty-five states.

An interloper to the Pacific Northwest U.S., Thorn stalks city streets, writes in cafes, loves live music, and talks to crows, squirrels, and trees.

Connect with Thorn:
www.thorncoyle.com